Highland

Sorcerer

Clover Autrey

This is a work of fiction. Names, characters, places, and incidents are either the product of the author's imagination or are used fictitiously, and any resemblance to actual persons living or dead, business establishments, events, or locales, is entirely coincidental

Published by Red Rover Books
Photos used to design cover were legally obtained from Period Images

ISBN 978-1470088200

To my grandkids
I truly do love you more than
A bushel and a peck

.

Highland Sorcerer

Charity Greves barely plunked her purse down on the counter when a mini-cyclone rippled through her kitchen, lifting her hair and zinging an electrical current down her spine. The world opened up on a slash of spiraling gray—and a naked bleeding man materialized out of thin air.

And dropped to the linoleum.

Hey. She just mopped that floor.

The gray swirling rift in space hovered above her kitchen sink for a few seconds, snatching at her clothing and hair, until it twisted and swirled and folded in on itself like a small universe imploding. Then poof, it was gone as though it had never been other than the lock of hair she swiped back from in front of her face.

She frowned. Sorcerer.

Had to be a sorcerer. They were the only magic wielders around who had the ability to open up a rift in space and travel its stormy interior from one place to another. The distance depended entirely upon the strength of magic a sorcerer had. In truth, odds were that taking a cab would get one here more quickly.

Yet this one, must be fairly powerful by the looks of him. Not that he looked powerful at all, but there weren't many sorcerers left in the world who could tune in and sense a healer across any distance and fewer still who could open and travel through a rift in space while in the weakened condition he appeared to be in.

Her pulse kicked up a notch. Should she be afraid? Backing up toward the door, she grabbed her cell phone to punch in 911, wondering just how dangerous the sorcerer could be, except…he didn't look all that dangerous sprawled on her floor, bleeding all over it. Kicked and battered puppy was more like it. And she was a healer who couldn't exactly explain how a naked guy ended up in her apartment in that condition if she called for help anyway. She needed to get a grip and take care of the man already.

He'd obviously come to her for help. Which was mildly flattering that someone within the magical community had actually heard of her for him to seek her out. The ads she and her sister had put out for the herbal shop must be paying off. Unless he had simply let his senses pick a healer out at random. Not as flattering a thought, but a gal had to take what she could get.

Charity pulled a stack of dish towels from a drawer and knelt down beside the poor guy. After all, it wasn't every day she came home from the herbal shop to have a wounded sorcerer travel across space especially for her world-renowned healing abilities.

Okay, so she wasn't world-renowned, and she'd only been sought out maybe three times before. At most. And one of those times was a sorcerer seeking her grandmother, but technicalities. She'd been present when he showed up so that counted.

"All right, big guy, what's going on with you?" She frowned, looking him over. His wounds were not of the stubbed-my-toe variety she realized, taking a closer look. He was really hurt, worse than she'd at first thought. He was covered in welts and gashes, blood and grime across his torso, hips and legs. Some of those cuts looked pretty deep. His eyes remained closed though the thick lashes fluttered with each pain-filled rise of his chest. His wrists were torn and chafed as though some kind of bindings had encircled them for a long time, some kind of thick band, not rope. Since nothing inorganic traveled through a space rift she couldn't be sure. Her muscles tightened. Someone had done this to him. Maybe she should call the police in.

Her stomach twisted, fear fighting with sympathy.

Whatever he'd endured, it had been horrible and her heart went out to him. What on earth had this sorcerer gotten himself into? And a more troubling thought: Would whatever he'd gotten himself into follow him here? She really didn't want to get into any magical squabbles within the wielder community.

"Okay, easy. I'm going to help you." She lifted his head off the floor to get a few of the folded dish towels beneath him and then smoothed a lock of sweaty dark hair off his cheek.

He flinched at the touch, eyes snapping open, and before she knew what happened, Charity was rolled onto her back with two hundred pounds of disoriented naked male on top of her, pinning her wrist against the floor.

"Ouch. Seriously?"

His gaze tracked around her kitchen, dark brows scrunching together at her shiny red trash compactor before settling back on her.

"Are ye the Healer Enchantress?" he rasped and promptly passed out. Right on top of her.

Charity's breath poured out in a whoosh. The guy was heavy. This close he didn't smell so great either which, considering the coating of dirt and sweat and blood, shouldn't be unexpected, but bleh. Well, this outfit was ruined.

She heaved out a breath, her stomach pushing up against his. Really? He was all muscle. Really heavy muscle. She pushed at his chest while at the same time tried to wriggle out from beneath him. He didn't budge. With his chin settled in the hollow between her neck and shoulder, his warm breath tickled her ear and his breathing pattern settled into sync with hers, stomach to stomach rising and falling together, which in other circumstances, all that lean male muscle over her would be...heat flushed her skin. She had to get him off of her because he was also hurt and losing blood and she needed to do her job and take care of him.

She pushed on his shoulders and wiggled her legs and hips to the side. Inch by inch, got her lower body at least out from beneath him until she finally got enough leverage to push his upper body over enough to roll him over off of her and onto his back. His arms flopped to his sides.

She sat up, breathing hard.

This was not going so well. And what was up with *Healer Enchantress*? The women in her family hadn't been called that for ages.

Charity crawled to kneel at the top of his head where it wouldn't be so easy for him to grab her again. She hoped. Even semi-conscious, the man had been quick.

Gently this time, she pressed another dish towel to the worse still-bleeding wound on his chest and tapped his cheek. "Hey mister. Uh, sorcerer. Guy." Nothing. She poked his shoulder. "I'd, um, go ahead and heal you, but, uh, you know it works better with a name. Soooo...if you wouldn't mind waking up again—more calmly this time? I really do want to help you." And let him get on his way to go do whatever sort of things sorcerers did. Which with the mistreated condition he was in probably wasn't something she wanted to know about either.

Not so much as a twitch from him.

Great.

Okay, then. She'd do this without his name. She stretched her hands wide over his chest. It really would be better to know who he was. Names held power. And he clearly needed her best aid. Especially since, well, she wasn't exactly the most skilled healer in the family even on her best day.

The thrumming started in the pit of her belly. Magic pulsed through her, the rustle of a flock of birds taking sudden flight. Buzzing energy surged upward and outward with each stroke of her heart, carrying forth the innate magic that was hers by birth and heritage.

Magic flowed through her, tingling and glowing beneath her skin like translucent static electricity. An icy chill swept through her arms first, her essence pushing the magic from deep within her core up through her blood stream. The ends of her hair lifted. Focused, Charity anchored the magic deep within her core and guided the power through her arms into her hands and outward...to flow into him. The one who needed her.

The sorcerer gasped. His back arched up, neck stretched. His shoulders and head ground into the floor, but she kept going, kept pouring the healing into him, even knowing she caused him pain.

Healing was never easy. Not for the one being healed nor for the one doing the healing.

The cuts on his flesh began mending, decreasing in size. The swollen skin around the bruises lightened. Tendrils of opaque pink light twisted between her fingers. Her head pinched, right behind her eye, ten times worse than a sinus ache. The man's eyes flared open. Piercing ice-blue. Large hands caught around Charity's wrists as though to hurl her hands from him, but instead his hold tightened.

"Toren," he panted out, eyes locked with hers. With the speaking of his name, magic flowed out of him, into her, forceful and hard. His magic. Sorcery.

That had never happened to her before.

Stunned, Charity shied back from it, until the awful quaking of his body tore at her healer's heart. She wouldn't stop now. Bearing down, she rode the tremendous wave of energy like a pebble rolling with a landslide.

She grasped onto his magic, adding it to her own, enhancing her limited supply with what he had in spades. The healing flowed from her like the pull of a tide, streaming into him, knitting flesh and bone faster than she would ever have managed on her own. Too fast. She wasn't sure she could contain it, guide it to where it needed to go. A rib moved beneath her palm. Calcium fused back together. She felt it bubble, shape and harden beneath their combined magic.

Their magic whipped around like a caged wind, seeking a vent. She flew deep inside him. She didn't mean to, it just kind of happened, like being sucked into a whirlpool of churning magic. She felt adrift in strong emotions. His. She swirled through them, a crumbling leaf in turbulent winds, but wow—he was beautiful. Or rather, his essence was beautiful. He was protective to the extreme. A man who bore the weight of responsibility like a glowing crown or halo on his head, streaked with determination and stubbornness. He was a man accustomed to making quick and lasting judgments—Charity tried to pull away from the emotions, not understanding how she knew all that about him in a mere instant. She just felt it. Experienced every emotion with him, all his hopes, wants. All his fears. And he loved. Her heart nearly exploded with the power of his love. Fiercely, with unfathomable kindness and compassion etched deeply into his soul. Pressure built behind her eyes. Her throat tightened. He…he…this was too much. Too much. In an instant, she understood this man better than she knew anybody, yet she didn't even know him at all. They'd just met. This was some deep and strange messed-up kind of magical energy going on between them.

His thoughts jumbled inside her head. He was

confused. Disoriented. And profoundly worried. About himself? No. Others. Others were in danger. He was determined to endure. Give them a chance...

Charity tried to break free of his turbulent emotions. She didn't understand them how this was happening, but they were so strong, dragging her under. She didn't want them. They were so powerful. He loved deeply and worried deeply, intoxicatingly so. She had to break away. Now. Or succumb to his feelings. She pulled back on her magic, dragging it away from his and felt the slide of his thoughts and sensations trickle away, fading from her head, her soul.

She could think a little more clearly now, nearly pulled out of him completely, but she hesitated. She still had a job to do. Breathing deeply, she turned her magic back and dove into the process of healing, searching for other injuries or illness. Another broken rib. Broken fingers. Torn ligaments in his shoulder. Who could do such a thing to someone like him?

Reining in her distress at his mistreatment, she worked efficiently even though she had never even attempted to heal so many injuries at once. Her magic would usually be at an end by now until she could rest and replenish what she'd used from the magic of the earth. But with the magic she had borrowed from him, she seemed to have an abundant supply so she kept going, healing as much as she could while she could.

That was the thing about magic. It could be shared between willing parties, though never just taken. However, even borrowed magic could still only be used in the medium of the magical wielder using it. Charity could draw from the sorcerer's reserves, yet that would not give her the abilities or skills of a sorcerer. She wouldn't be able to throw fire balls or open rifts in the cosmos. The only thing she could do with it is heal. And it worked the other way around too. If the sorcerer drew upon her magic, small as it was, his would be enhanced, but he still would not have the gift of healing.

So he had sought her out.

She and her sister shared magic every now and then, and they'd both helped their grandmother when she healed a few of the more extreme injuries, but she'd never once experienced this sharing of emotions before. Which...the flow of healing abruptly stopped seeking for wounds as she was struck by a disturbing thought. Could he be experiencing her emotions right now as well? She didn't want a stranger—a sorcerer at that—knowing her so intimately.

And it was intimate.

Think on that later. There's nothing you can do about it now. Heal him while you still have strength, her inner voice reasoned. She resumed the current of his magic, moving to another second broken rib. This was going to hurt. She readied for it, yet the pain of mending bone clawed at her throat and with the healing came images—sensations. Not the emotions again, but a full-on viewing.

She groaned. She heard the echo of it from outside her body as though it came from someone else.

She'd never had a viewing before either. It wasn't exactly what healers did. Healers, well, healed. Plain and simple.

Images flooded her mind like looking through the long cylinder of a telescope and zooming in with the lens. She glimpsed a woman at the other end, features indistinct and hazy. And then she was there in a darkened room beside the woman. Like she'd been propelled to another place. Toren was there too, standing, his back against a stone wall. Leather bands with glowing gold markings secured his wrists to the wall. His head hung down. Dark hair obscured his face, yet Charity knew it was him. She felt the unique signature of his magic pouring off of him.

She watched the scene around her as though she were a specter inside the room with them. The sorcerer really was a prisoner. The leather bands had caused all the damage to his poor wrists. It was archaic, completely surreal. Okay, there were a lot of magic wielders who were just plain nuts, but seriously, who did things like this? The woman's long nails grazed over Toren's bare chest, and Charity stiffened.

Without thinking, Charity grabbed for the lady's arm to stop her, but her hand passed right through. Because, oh yeah, she wasn't really there. This was all just an instant replay of scenes from Toren's brain she got a front row seat for while she was in the process of healing him. A healing that had been interrupted by a viewing. This was so weird. She wished it would stop, that this motion picture would shut off.

Toren moaned, trying to lift his head. Firelight flickered across his sweat-dampened skin. She wrinkled her nose at the scent of smoke and pitch.

A tattered plaid kilt slanted low across his waist in contrast to the woman's pristine white gown. They looked like they'd stepped onto a historical movie set. The woman placed her palm to the wounded sorcerer's ribcage. Her lips moved. As though it possibly made any difference, Charity leaned forward, concentrating on the words.

"...will be mine...hidden..."

That's all she got before the woman pressed her palm forward and Toren's ribs snapped. The punch of it speared through Charity. She flinched back—screamed out the pain. Toren's head flung back against the hard wall. His eyes rolled back in agony.

Charity fell forward, wrenched violently back through the looking glass, her sight tunneled in rapid force back to her kitchen and one hand slapped against the floor, the other on Toren's chest at exactly the same spot the witch's hand had been above his ribs.

Crap!

Charity jerked her hand away.

The sorcerer's magic abruptly abandoned her.

She listed a little sideways before catching herself. A tingly floaty sensation assailed her. The spot behind her eye felt like a pencil had drilled through it. She felt dizzy like when you stand up too fast. The edges of her vision dimmed, her typical physical reaction after a healing. It drained her. She could expect the sinus headache to hit with full force into a migraine in about twenty minutes and then she'd need to sleep it off for several hours. Except this headache seemed to be already pounding against her skull a little faster than usual.

Toren hissed, eyes fever-bright against flushed skin, and locked on hers with a silent plea.

She pushed her own concerns aside for now. She needed to attend to him quickly and see him on his way while she was still functional. Before her headache was too much for her to even move. That woman in white had hurt him. Had been hurting him for who knew how long? How could someone do that?

"Shhh-shh." Charity ran a trembling palm across Toren's brow. During the healing, or rather that connection between them, she'd felt his pain and vulnerability as well as the hope he'd so desperately clung onto in the midst of horrific torture. As much as she didn't appreciate the intrusion, she also had never wanted to help anyone more than she did this man. It burned into her like a physical need. She had to help him however she could. She was going to help him. "I'm going to fix this."

Still staring at her, his lips quirked up in a sad smile and all sorts of things started leaping around in Charity's belly. Her chest constricted. She stared. Her mouth went dry. When he smiled like that, his face came alive. Even with the coating of dirt cracking around the lines at the corners of his eyes, he was breathtaking.

A warm palm slid around her wrist, his long fingers encircling it completely. "Ye already have." His voice was petal soft. Weak. Foreign.

"I've healed your injuries, but that woman...?" She could barely speak around the shock of what his mere smile was doing to her insides. Or maybe it was just an effect of the dizzying weakness creeping over her. She shook her head to try and clear it and get back to business. Which was a mistake. The pain behind her eye intensified. She forced herself to pull away from Toren's gaze and take a quick inventory. Bruises lingered where cuts and welts had been. Skin tone, though sweaty, held a healthy hue. She could feel his penetrating eyes watching her. She swallowed, trying to get moisture back in her mouth and felt along his ribcage, finding no give or unnatural movement.

Where that horrible witch had hurt him, Charity had healed. Her heart roared to life. The pain in her head seemed to soften with the victory. She'd done that?

She'd done that!

"*Yes*." She fist-pumped the air and immediately regretted the movement as a fresh spike of pain ripped through her head. No more fist-pumping for a while, but she couldn't stop the swell of excitement. All those injuries, all at once. She had never mended anything more serious than a light case of inflammation on her own before and that had exhausted her.

Toren shifted up a bit to lean back on his elbows. She felt him watching her. A quick glance proved it. She wished he would smile again. But why would he under the circumstances? She inhaled a calming breath. She better get it together. He'd been held prisoner, beaten, probably starved, somehow escaped and sought her out. She was probably the first healer his magic latched onto. He was still so weak.

She needed to act like a professional. Yes, she felt like she knew him. Really well. Like she'd known him forever. But the truth was that she didn't. They weren't friends. They weren't acquaintances. They weren't anything, but well, now healer and patient, she supposed. Poor guy still looked like he'd gone ten rounds in a meat grinder. She needed to stop thinking of him as someone she knew and be the professional healer.

Food. She needed to get something in him before he passed out on her, maybe some soup. She could use some as well. Or tea. Definitely let him use her shower and get him something to wear, though even her baggiest sweats weren't going to fit. She had a blanket. He should be used to that. After all he had been wearing a kilt when she had the vision of him in that dungeon.

A kilt?

Dungeon.

Torchlight.

Healer Enchantress.

"Oh my...." She slapped a hand across her mouth, those tiny details settling into her weary overwhelmed and pounding mind. Her other hand started flapping.

"Oh my oh my you…you..."

She was so stupid, so caught up in the euphoria of being sought out and then actually healing. No wonder she'd been able to do it—with the kind of power this sorcerer had.

His magic had to be beyond immense if what she was thinking was true.

Could it be?

Was that even possible?

"Where are you from?" Her voice came out like a breathless whisper.

His head canted to the side, dark brows bunching, the picture of innocence.

Charity swallowed past the hysteria climbing her throat and tried again. "When? When are you from?" floor.

Chapter Two

Charity fell back on her butt.

Toren's gaze tracked around her kitchen, the lighting and modern appliances, then back to her. "Your past. I believe."

The past. And he wasn't talking like a-week-ago-last-Wednesday past. No, the guy was a full-on sorcerer powerful enough to not just transport himself through space rifts across far distances—but through time as well.

At least several centuries worth, if not more. Holy freaking cow.

Her chest lifted in rapid pants, squeezing air from her lungs. She was going to hyperventilate. Might as well go with it. The massive healing had already taken a lot out of her anyway. Passing out would be for the best. She'd wake up and the time traveler would be gone. Poof. Back to his own time and—

"Lass, are ye well?"

Lass. He said *"lass"*. And *"ye"*. Ohcrapohcrapohcrap.

She inhaled a deep breath, let it out slowly and

nodded.

He smiled encouragingly, coaxing her to relax. *Ah man*. Don't smile like that. Do not smile. It was hard enough to think as it was. Her head was pounding, her stomach dropping, slowing to her toes. She was going to throw up. She knew it.

Get it together, Greves. So he's a sorcerer from the past. It happens, right? He'd suffered torture, broken bones, traveled through a time rift that it must have taken an inordinate amount of magic to open, especially considering he'd have to have bypassed those spelled bands with the glowing symbols holding him prisoner to a dungeon wall. *A dungeon wall*. She pressed her fingers to her pounding temples.

He endured the agony of a quick healing—was too exhausted to drag his naked self off the floor—yet he was making sure she was all right. She needed to just suck it up and pull herself together.

Some healer she was.

"Okay, okay. I got this." Shaking, she blew out another breath, steadied herself against a sudden wave of dizziness, and flipped her hair out of her eyes. "Soup. No, tea. I'll put on some tea." She got up, spinning about the small space, much too fast. She grabbed onto the counter and let the bout of weakness pass before she grabbed up the tea pot and shoved it under the faucet. "Would you like some tea?" The water tinkled into the pot.

He watched her warily, sitting there on her floor, hands propped behind him. His nose crinkled, making little creases in the dirt dusting his skin as though he hadn't had anything to smile about in a long time before he'd come here. Of course he hadn't smiled. He'd been pinned to a freaking dungeon wall.

Charity's hands shook when she flipped on the electronic water boiler and set it to heat. What was she doing, leaving a poor exhausted sorcerer on the floor?

She sighed, hesitant to get near him now that he'd been healed and she'd shared in his memories—and wow, that had been...wow.

Stop it. Get a grip. She was his caregiver at the moment so she'd better start giving care.

Stiffening her spine, she turned back to him and those eyes drew her right in. A startling bright blue flecked with soft gold. They were intense. That little something fluttered in her belly again. She did not need this.

"Here. Let's get you cleaned up."

She stooped low in front of him to get her arms beneath his and her gaze dipped then snapped back up to his face.

"Um, hang on." She went into the living area to grab the chamois blanket off the back of the sofa. A battering ram was banging against her skull.

He was standing when she spun back around.

"I can manage." His soft burr held amusement.

"Uh-huh. Okay, yeah." She shoved the blanket at him. He grabbed it. Smooth muscles rolled beneath the grimy arm when he pressed the blanket to his stomach and left it dangling. He was way taller than he'd looked on the floor. The top of his head brushed the arched doorway between rooms. Charity's legs turned to rubber.

"Shower's this way."

He squinted. Oh yeah, medieval guy. "Bathroom." What did they call them? Did Scotsmen even bathe in anything besides lakes back then? "Uh, garderobe?"

"Bath room." The bland expression clearly

conveyed he wasn't an idiot. "A chamber for bathing. Aye."

Yep. She'd insulted him.

"Sorry."

He smiled, showing a hint of white teeth this time. The tingly feeling in her belly increased. He had to stop doing that.

Apparently history was wrong on a whole lot of hygienic habits or Toren came from great calcium-enriched stock, which going by his size wasn't too hard to believe.

They stood there awkwardly facing each other. Charity waited for him to make a move to follow her. He lifted a shaky hand and tottered.

"Oh hey." Charity sprang forward, ignoring the wobble to her own step and placed a hand to his chest, the other at his back to steady him. The muscles beneath her palm tightened as his arm draped over her shoulder. He leaned into her, though she suspected he didn't give her his full weight, which was good since she was about to go down any minute in a heap of exhaustion.

"Ye have my gratitude, Lady."

She maneuvered him past the sofa and into

her small bathroom. "Charity."

"Charity." Her name rolled deliciously along his accent. "Clan Limont is in your debt, Lady Charity."

"The entire clan?" She grinned, trying to hide the fact that she was completely unnerved by his height and muscle tone and beautiful smile...and all those emotions she knew he carried deep down inside him. "And I'm not a lady. It's just Charity."

He sagged against her more heavily and she guided him onto the closed toilet seat. The bathroom seemed considerably smaller as she stepped between his legs to turn the spray on her shower/tub combination.

Toren leaned forward to study the flowing water. Reaching out, he cupped a hand beneath the spray and let it trickle between his fingers. Dirt immediately turned the stream of water falling from his hand a light brown.

"'Tis warm." His voice held all the wonder of a three-year-old seeing his first gumball dispenser.

Charity's chest tightened and she had the sudden urge to show him all the modern conveniences in her house and witness his eyes light up at the beep of her microwave or flush of the toilet or fizzle upon popping open a soda can. Talk about sensory overload. She rethought the idea. Better be careful. Poor guy had never even seen a movie. Just the ring of a cell phone could really freak him out.

For now, get him clean. "Want to get in?"

His nod was so eager, Charity laughed. "All right then."

Still too weak to stand for a long time, she helped him get into the tub, blanket and all, and lean back where he immediately closed his eyes. Long lashes blended with the smudges across his cheekbones. It was the most peaceful she'd seen him yet.

She slid onto the toilet seat lid, grateful to sit down and just breathed in and out for a while, letting the dizziness from getting him into the tub subside to a faint lightheadedness. Her limbs were dead weights.

Her bathroom contained an assortment of soaps, lotions, shampoos and conditioners in an array of containers and baskets—all test products, some created by herself for the herbal shop she and Lenore owned.

Most of the dirt was off Toren, the water running clearer down the drain, so she pushed the stopper down and turned off the shower's spray and let the faucet run to fill up the tub.

Wanting something gentle, yet also with added healing properties, she squeezed her favorite blend of liquid soap into a wash cloth and went to work.

The Highlander didn't so much as flinch, trusting her ministrations. Charity's heart gave a tender little pull. After what he'd endured in the dungeon, she was amazed he could trust anyone.

He sighed, pulling her from her troubled thoughts. She poured her favorite shampoo into her hands and began lathering his long hair.

One blue eye opened to squint at her. "Ye intend to have me smell of flowers?"

"Blue Tansy actually and any scent will be an improvement."

His lips twitched at that and Charity's mouth went dry. With most of the blood and dirt gone, she took a long look at him while rinsing the shampoo. She wouldn't call him exceptionally handsome, not in a pretty boy sort of way at any rate. But there was something about him, something rugged and masculine that called to the woman within her.

Or it could be that he was clean and sleekly muscled and naked and he'd traveled across space and time to seek her gift as a Healer Enchantress… Plus she knew him. Really knew him. She'd felt all the things that were important to him. And frankly, she hadn't been sure guys like him really existed. Not in her century at least.

She turned the water back, moving his head under the spray to the best advantage to rinse out the shampoo.

Toren's eyes flew open and then tightened. He curled over. His hand splayed across his stomach.

She slapped off the spray.

"What is it? Are you still hurt?"

Had she missed something during the healing?

His jaw clenched. "She's pulling me back."

"What? The woman who beat you?" Charity grabbed onto his arm as though that could keep him there. "Can't you stop it? Close off the rift somehow?"

Which…shouldn't a rift be opening? How was the awful woman pulling him back? Only sorcerers had power over a rift. And sorcerers were always male. At least any she'd ever heard of. She'd assumed the woman had been a witch with how she'd broken his ribs with magic.

The charms. The glowing runes on his bands. They were back in time attached to the stone wall, but maybe they still held power over Toren though he was here. Maybe a rift didn't have to be opened. But, oh my, sucked back through time without one? That couldn't be good.

He shook his head tightly as though the smallest movement caused him great pain. His hand gripped the rim of the tub.

Charity clutched her own fingers over his to anchor him to the here and now. The thought of him being yanked back to that horrible woman's clutches terrified her. But he was spelled to those bands. Just because he could slip out of them traveling through time, they were still spelled to him. She knew it, felt the knowledge sift through from his memories. "Just hold onto me. Stay here."

Agonized eyes locked onto hers. "'Tis not possible." His hand flexed beneath her palm, rock hard, riding out the terrible pull on his body.

How much could one man go through?

She didn't want him to go back to that. Not to a woman who would just hurt him all over again. He didn't deserve that. He was too kind. Too honorable and protective. Protective. He endured the torture for someone else. She felt that, though he'd buried it deep.

"Yes it is. Anything is possible. Just fight it."

His hand slipped from beneath hers and he brought both palms up to her cheeks. They were callused and wet, but Charity didn't care. Her head pounded. There was a rawness to Toren's voice that scattered shivers across her arms. "Ye've helped me, Lady Charity. Ye've given me a blessed reprieve so I've the strength now to keep fighting. D'ye understand?"

No she did not understand. Her throat closing, she couldn't answer. She didn't want him to go. She wanted to help him. She'd never wanted anything more in her life. Nothing seemed as important.

She nodded, his hands moving with her movements, fingers curled in her hair. His jaw clenched, his chin lowered to his chest, bearing down on a wave of pain. His form flickered in and out like an old television on the fritz.

That had to hurt. On a cellular level. Would he even make it back in one piece?

"No, no, Toren, stay. Hold on. We'll think of something."

He was losing. His lips were clamped tight. The veins in his neck and forehead bulged.

She couldn't stop this.

Charity grabbed onto his wrists, sought deep within her center and pulled. She dived for every ounce of her healing power, everything that made her who she was, the divine feminine within her— her gift and her strength. It roared through her with an intensity born of desperation—blistering and feral—which she clamped down on and controlled, riding the current like a wild animal that she flung out, releasing everything she had to pour into the man.

If she couldn't keep him here, she could at least give him the last bit of her magic to give him the strength to endure.

A surge of wind tunneled through the bathroom, whipping the shower curtain and hanging towels.

Eyes wide, Toren's head jerked back. "What are you—?" He gasped, every muscle in his body going rigid, chest expanding on a pain-filled inhalation, dark wet hair lifting in the frenzied charged atmosphere.

"Charity—" he screamed on a gush of breath, his form blurring.

He disappeared beneath her grasp and her hands whipped out, closing around air.

The wind died. Water splashed out of the faucet. Throbbing pain pounded inside her head.

Sapped of strength, Charity slumped to the floor.

Chapter Three

Toren hurdled out of the air back inside the dungeon. He dropped to the floor, hands splayed across the grainy stone. His entire body ached like he'd been wrung through a sieve. The hated bands materialized instantly around his wrists, the bespelled symbols he had so painstakingly unraveled for days to make his brief escape, glowed even more brilliantly than before—strengthened in tri-fold measure. He would not be able to so easily slip their bonds again. At least he wasn't pinned to the hated wall.

The swirl of soft fabric rustled near. The hem of Aldreth's white gown floated across his fingers as the witch crouched near his shoulders.

"Clever, clever sorcerer."

Slender fingers stroked his wet hair. "You've bathed." She caressed the back of his shoulders. He stiffened, vowing when he had these bands off, he'd wrap his hands around her dainty little throat. "And have endured a healing. I see. Ye fled to a Healer Enchantress then? Was it worth the cost, young Limont? To have your perfect bones rejoined

39

that I might have the pleasure of breaking them all over again? Mended flesh that I might once again peel away? Ye believe with this healing ye've gained the strength and will to endure, but I remind you how many long lonely years I have lived, how patient I can be. You will break in time and I will have what I seek."

Though it took every reserve he had in him, Toren lifted his head to face her in challenge. "Ye need my acceptance to retrieve it." He grinned in defiance and hoped he did it well. "I'll die before giving you that."

Bending down in front of him, she cupped his chin between her palms and frowned. "I suppose ye will." Abruptly she removed her hands and let his head fall. Toren barely caught himself before his forehead hit the stone.

Aldreth rose and paced away. The hem of her gown swept along the filthy floor. "'Twould not be my favored outcome. Ye know I prefer you to your brothers."

Every muscle in Toren's body stiffened. She had used the threat to his family before, yet it still punched a hole through his gut every time. He prayed Shaw and Col remained safely shrouded and didn't try anything stupid—like coming after him.

Toren pushed up on his hands, arms shaking. Aldreth was a fool if she thought threatening his younger siblings would have the desired effect. It only strengthened his resolve to hold out longer and give them time to take the clan to the standing stones of *Reolin Skene* and remove their magic from Aldreth's reach permanently.

Aldreth clapped her hands together. "I wonder if Shaw will hold out as long as ye. So young for a sorcerer, his powers barely honed, I cannot imagine he will endure more than a sennight. Shall we wager? I can bring him here. 'Twas so simple to trick you. Think ye I cannot capture another Limont as easily?"

Toren roared, pulling himself to his knees. "Witch. Ye will not touch my brother."

Skirts swirling, Aldreth crouched near again. Her finger stroked down his nose. "This does not have to be difficult. We could be powerful together. Ye'll see. I'm not evil, Toren. I will not harm your people. I will not harm your precious siblings. That is not what I seek for them."

"The very essence of what ye propose will harm them."

"Nay. 'Twill make them free. 'Twill give them more power than you have ever considered. Think on this—your brother, the shifter—"

Toren froze. *Col.*

"If ye gave in to the full potential of the magic we could wield between us, it would flow through the entire clan, as your clan's magic flows to you. Your brother could hold another form for several nights on end, not groveling just to hold shape for the mere hours that exhausts him. All the shifters could. And think of the attributes for your seers and storm summoners, the water-called and moon-touched. Notwithstanding the power you could acquire for yourself unrestrained as a sorcerer. Do you not desire to feel that strength run through you? I do not understand why ye resist our blending of magic. 'Twould make us both stronger, more potent. 'Twould make the clan stronger. 'Tis a blessing that should not go to waste."

"Which would become a curse and well ye know it. There's too much darkness in ye. Demon

42

born magic, Aldreth. You've colluded with demons, taken oaths to them. I want no part in that. My clan will have no part in that. What ye propose is madness."

"'Tis power."

"'Tis wrong."

"Coward. The lot of ye. An entire clan of cowards. Reach out and seize what's yours. I offer you that."

"Ye offer naught but shadows and death for all of Limont. We've seen this before. We know what happens to those who take upon too much magic that isn't inherently their own. Darkness, Aldreth, like the darkness that rides upon your blackened soul."

"What ye call dark, I call liberation."

"Aye, the liberation of all vows to duty."

That hit a nerve. Aldreth yanked his head back like a striking serpent. "Vows are meant to be broken. Think on that, sorcerer. My grandsire had the courage to challenge the Fae and unleash the magic upon the land. All magic."

"Magic that was given freely from those he challenged. The Fae are right to have guardians to balance what they have given. 'Tis an honorable covenant and blessing bestowed upon our kind. Your grandsire was mad to believe that magic has no need of protectors."

"Then protect magic. Do your duty. With me. Who better suited than a daughter of Alduein blended with the son of Limont? Together. Our magic will be the most potent blend the land has ever witnessed."

Toren closed his eyes. A daughter of the clan first deemed as magic protectors whose High Sorcerer turned on the Fae as a hound turned on its master. 'Twas a sorrowful day to all magic born when Burnes Alduein fell and the entire clan was banished. And these centuries later, the wee granddaughter returned grown to take back what she believed was rightfully hers. A powerful witch in her own right, but her magic was tainted. All could feel the underscore of darkness obscured within her essence. Should Toren or any of his siblings join their magic with hers, the scale between light and dark would be unbalanced, throwing their world into an unimaginable night where darkness overshadowed everything.

He could not give her what she sought without severing his oaths and dooming all earth magic to the balance of darkness. The world would be overrun by creatures best left skimming the shadows.

"Nay, Aldreth, joining with you would be the breaking of all I hold dear."

She hissed and slammed his face into the stone floor. He felt bones in his cheek crack, nearly going blind with the pain.

She swung away and threw the dirty plaid at him. "Then rot here until ye've changed your mind. And give him a shave," she tossed to the guard waiting outside the dungeon. "I despise hair-roughened skin."

Her clipped steps marched across the floor just before the heavy wooden door creaked and banged shut, splashing him in moldy darkness.

Chapter Four

"I can't believe it. One of the fabled sorcerers of Limont came to you. In the flesh."

"In nothing but his flesh." Charity helped her sister haul the ancient tome down from the second highest shelf. As self-appointed keeper of their family's knowledge, Lenore's dining nook-turned-library was wall-to-wall flea market book cases cramped with books, texts, even scrolls that museum curators would give their eyeteeth for.

Together they carried the heavy tome between them and laid it on the table that took up the center of the room.

"You sure it's in here?" Charity eyed the large book dubiously.

"Oh yeah, I remember reading about it when I first convinced mom to let me look at the book."

"You were ten."

Lenore shrugged with one shoulder. "It was a romantic story. An entire clan, every individual gifted with some form of magic as long as they remained the protectors of man...and then all of them vanished. Poof. The village must have fallen to ruin because no one knows where it once was." She opened the little ornately carved box she kept sitting on the table and pulled out the white gloves she kept in there. Lenore was meticulous about not letting the oils in her fingers damage any of the ancient books.

"That's so weird." Charity sat down and leaned over the large velum pages that Lenore turned with delicate reverence. "What does that even mean? Protectors of man?"

"Got me. Something about the innate balance of magic. As long as the Limonts kept the dark side of magic from overtaking the light, and vice versa, the entire land would prosper. Magic would remain abundant and the flip side of magic, like the dark fairies, ghouls and vampires wouldn't get more than their share of a foothold in the world. Neither would overpower the other. With the protectors and their clan in place, magic would remain balanced. Here it is." Lenore tapped a page and slipped her black reading glasses on.

Charity scooted her chair closer so that their heads were side by side. Celtic writing wasn't exactly her forte. Their grandmother had insisted that as practicing healers, both girls at least know enough to pick out runes and symbols for spells and incantations in several nearly dead languages. Charity could get by, but her younger sister's huge brain excelled in it.

She scanned down what looked like a listing of names—genealogical records with years and, wow, magical abilities. Her heart jolted when she came to his name. "Toren Limont," she whispered, making her encounter with him seem that much more surreal. "High Sorcerer of Limont, born in Crunfathy." Her breathing stilled, frozen in her chest. An ancient wounded Highlander really had flung himself through time to seek her aid, and then he was gone—to a place she couldn't reach him or help him. The urge to somehow help him consumed her every thought since he had come to her. After she came to by the tub, she hadn't been able to sleep all night. Her thoughts replayed everything that had passed between them and the more she thought of him, the more urgent the feeling to help him grew. "Have you ever heard of Crunfathy?"

"Just in this text. Nowhere else. It's been lost to

human history, as though magic never existed."
Lenore's fingers swept over hers. "You okay?"

"Yeah. It's just weird, you know?"

"Do you want to stop?"

"No, I want to know what happened." She needed to know. She didn't understand it, but since she'd healed Toren, saw what he'd gone through, felt his resolve; she desperately needed to know that he was okay. She frowned. Who was she kidding? It was more than that. She knew the man, knew him better than she knew anyone. She had felt his inner essence, everything that made him *him.* From what irritated him to what he held dear. With the healing, he had somehow gotten deep under her skin as though he were almost a part of her now. She was going to find out what happened to him and his story had better end up being a happy one or else…or else what? What could she do about anything? She'd healed him and he'd gone back to where he belonged. That was that. That was all it could ever be. Right?

Right?

No that wasn't right. He didn't belong in a dungeon.

She had to know if he escaped, and if not, she had to help him somehow. She couldn't stop thinking about helping him. She had to help him.

Which was monumentally stupid to dwell so much on, considering whatever the outcome with the terrible woman who was torturing him, Toren Limont was still centuries long dead.

None of it mattered now. Except it did.

"All right." Lenore was back in research mode—all business with her glasses sliding down her little nose. She'd twisted her Faerie-soft blond hair on top of her head out of the way, slipping a pencil in the knot to hold it in place. "Your Toren was the last known sorcerer before the clan vanished for good. You see these other names below his?"

Charity squinted, her belly taking a tumble at the word *vanished*.

Lenore traced the names with the tip of a gloved finger.

Toren Limont

Shaw Limont

Edeen Limont

Col Limont

"He had two brothers and a sister. It looks like that together the four siblings kept their people safe and the balance of magic in check. They also..." Lenore's eyes lit up. "They also each had their own unique brand of magic. The sister was an empath."

"She could tap into other people's emotions."

"Yes, but back then when magic was part of everyday existence and so much stronger, an empath would have been able to do way more than feel emotions. We're talking the ability to really get into people's heads, dive into memories they don't even know about if she wanted to."

"Seriously? So if she touched one of us, she'd see everything we know?"

"Yes. Can you imagine our healing potential if we lived back then? Magic was in everything, as simple as plucking it from the air." Lenore's smile was bright, excited.

Charity could very well imagine the potential. She'd experienced the power of Toren's magic firsthand, had tapped into its strength and healed him as easily as a thought. And had somehow ended up inside his essence, probably very much like what an Empath would experience. She wasn't sure she'd want that ability on her hands, not with everyone. She'd experienced it with Toren and now she couldn't stop thinking about him.

Granted, Toren was Toren, an amazingly rare person, who was so honorable and good, and…crap, she had it bad.

Great. She had to go and fall for a long-dead sorcerer, protector of all magic, chieftain of an entire clan. Talk about going for a guy who was way out of reach. Just what she needed.

Lenore chatted on, the deep-seeded learner in her charging ahead full bore. "So your Toren was the sorcerer, Edeen an empath. The youngest brother, Col, was a shapeshifter, and Shaw—" Lenore's nose wrinkled and her glasses slipped down farther. "Moon sifter."

"Which is?"

"I have no idea." But Lenore's lips puckered outward in that way that meant she was determined to find out. "So now you know. Your visitor really was a Highland sorcerer, last of his line before the entire Clan Limont vanished and magic hasn't been as potent on the earth since. It's all pretty amazing when you think about it."

"Yeah." Charity sighed. "Amazing."

"Hey." Lenore reached over and pushed stray wisps of dark hair behind Charity's ear. "It is amazing. It's not every day things like this happen."

"I know."

"You did what you could for him. And you got to feel incredible power flow through you, more than either of us could generate in these days. That had to feel awesome, right? I know it's hard when you heal someone. You feel like you're responsible for them, but there's nothing more you can do. It's not like you can travel back through time and check on him."

Charity's gaze snapped up. That's exactly what she wanted to do. "We have time-travel spells. Grandma's done it." Healers couldn't open time and space rifts like a sorcerer could, but when a healer's emotions were focused strongly enough on helping someone else, there were spells and formulas that could do the trick for very short stretches across time. Very short. A few hours, possibly a day to help someone avoid an accident or illness that a healer didn't have the magical strength to heal. The connection between healer and patient had to be very strong, very motivated. The emotions on high-voltage.

Lenore pulled her glasses off. "She went back half a day to stop Uncle Frank from getting in that car accident that took his leg. Even if you could pull it off, what would be the point in going back to last night and your Highlander? You've already done what you can for him. It's not like we have the ability or spells to travel across centuries. Not even the sorcerers of today have the juice to do that anymore."

Frowning, Charity glared down at the open pages.

"I'm sorry," Lenore said. "I get it, but it's not possible so there's no use in worrying about him anymore. Whatever happens—*happened*—to Toren Limont is out of your hands. You got to just let it go."

"I know, okay." Charity got up and pulled her grandmother's little pink book of spells from one of the lower shelves, the book she knew had the time-travel incantations. "I'm going to take this home, all right?"

"Sure." Lenore's lips puckered out again. "Just don't...you know."

"Like you said, no one has the juice to travel back that far anyway."

Chapter Five

T oren lay in the dungeon, his cheek against the cold stone exactly where the mercenaries had left him after shaving him raw. At least she had left him alone without starting immediately back in with her whips, or worse, her magical tortures.

She was right, even with the recent healing, he wouldn't be able to endure much longer.

He stared at the enchanted band on his wrist, feeling the frustration of no choices as deeply as the exhaustion enveloping his body.

He could goad her into outright killing him, but then her attention would be turned to his siblings. Nay, he had to continue as long as he could to give them a chance to flee. If they hadn't already. There was no way to know.

He was just so achingly bone-weary.

Squeezing his eyes closed, Toren drifted away, allowing sleep to bolster the reviving energies the little healer of the future had gifted him with.

At the last moment before Aldreth had pulled him back, the young healer thrust everything she had into him. It hadn't been anywhere near the amount needed to restore what Aldreth had bled from him, yet Toren was touched that the maiden would give him all that she had.

Toren escaped to sleep with the swirl of a name on his lips. *Charity*.

He knew her. Somehow during her healing, a connection between them had been forged. He knew all the depths and layers to this woman of the future and marveled at the sweetness that existed in her demeanor. She hoped deeply and loved powerfully. Family meant everything to her. She would dive into the murkiest waters to protect them.

A faint smile curved his lips in sleep. He'd had nothing to smile about for so long, yet the lass had managed to coax several from him.

She came to him then—in his dreams—all creamy skin and lustrous dark hair. He'd wanted to feel the softness of it when he'd first seen her but coming as a beggar in search of a Healer Enchantress's aid, he had refrained.

But he walked in the dreamworld now and she but a manifestation conjured by his mind.

She ran to him, across the moor, mist curling

at her hips, teasing cloudy swirls around her breech-covered legs until she stood before him, slender hands upon his crisp white shirt.

"Toren," she breathed.

He smiled at the unusual inflection she gave to his name and since she was but a dream, he indulgently dragged his fingers into her hair, sighing at the silkiness that was softer than he'd anticipated.

"Toren, I need you to tell me where you are. I'm going to help you."

What's this? Toren grazed the back of his knuckles along her cheek. His dream conjured enchantress shouldn't look so troubled.

He wanted her to be pleasant, pliant, a lovely peaceful memory to hold on to, to focus his mind on during the worst of what Aldreth would surely bring. He didn't know how long he'd be given uninterrupted sleep and he intended to make the most of it. Toren willed his dream to fall into order, arranging his thoughts so that the focused lines above Lady Charity's pert little nose would smooth.

Her lips tightened in exasperation. "Toren, focus please. Tell me where you are. Where is the dungeon? Within a castle? Tell me how to free you."

Toren pulled back, holding her at arm's length to really get a good look at her. Impatience and sharp intelligence stared back through disarming violet eyes, filled with far too much life to be a dream-induced manifestation.

"Are ye dream-trailing?"

Dainty shoulders hitched up in a shrug. "I'd just gone to bed, now I'm here." She fluttered her hands. "But I know enough to realize that sometimes truths that you normally can't see in the light of day will come to the surface in your dreams. I took an entire course on dream analysis once. Well maybe not a course, more like a weekend workshop. Anyway I figure since I'm dreaming about you I may as well be direct and ask you what I want to know. Who is that horrible woman? She's a witch, isn't she? Has to be a witch. Nobody else could hold a sorcerer. And those spelled bands… Where is she keeping you and how do I get you out?"

She was talking rapidly about things she couldn't possibly have any hand in and all Toren wanted to do was silence those lips with his own. The blood in his veins heated, dropped below the waist of his kilt. Toren clasped her hands between his in an attempt to stop her from rambling since her fingers twirled and gestured to emphasize every word. The only thing certain was that she was real and believed him to be the dream.

His lip quirked up, pleased that she would deem to dream of him at all, especially after the state he'd come to her in.

"Charity." Hands still within his, he brought her finger to his lips and kissed each tip. That brought her ramblings to a quick end. She blinked owlishly up at him as his lips moved from one finger to the next. Her breasts lifted on the swell of a breath and everything in Toren went quiet. He stared at her over her hand at his mouth. *Déithe*, she was lovely, her soul brimming with a passion he yearned to explore.

He spoke to her simply to distract him from the dishonorable thought of taking her here and now within a dream when she had merely come to help him. "Ye are dream-trailing. We both are. You're here. I'm here."

She opened her mouth to say something, then closed it, then opened it again, but only swallowed. Then blinked again. The flit of emotion filing across her face was mesmerizing. He could watch her for an eternity and never tire. Pulling a hand out from between his, she poked his arm. "You're real?"

He grinned. "As real as the part of me that can travel to the realm of dreams."

She jabbed him again. "So you're not real."

He recaptured her hand. "I'm real enough to feel that..." As well as other more potent things. "...so cease, though in truth my flesh and blood sleeps in Aldreth's dungeon."

Her eyes narrowed like a hawk that just spotted prey. Cunning little hunter. "Aldreth is the witch? Where is she keeping you?"

So she was back to that again. "Shhh, 'tis naught ye can do from centuries beyond mine. Forget about me." He tugged her hand, bringing her closer where she stared up at him with those huge beguiling eyes. "My time is finished before yours ever begins."

"But I can help. I can do something."

Her earnestness sailed straight to his heart,

melting the protective fortifications. What bride price he would pay to be free to pursue a woman like her. Nay, not like her. Her. If his circumstances were not doomed, he would travel through time again to make her his own. Ah, the fanciful musings of a weary, beaten soul. He was dreaming like a love-struck youth. Yet dreams were beyond him now. He had this dream, this one moment where they both happened to think of each other at the same moments to dream-trail together. 'Twas a rare occurrence and not likely to happen again so he would remember this time with her, cherish the promise of violet eyes and a gentle soul and pray that would be enough to sustain him for the coming trials Aldreth would put him through. "Ye have helped me. More than ye know."

"But your entire—" She looked away as she worked her bottom lip between her teeth.

Ah. He understood. She'd been about to tell him something of his future. 'Twould be easy for her to have searched the histories of his people and find out what had become of him and for a moment the temptation to ask how his clan fared ran great. But knowing could be a danger as well, could unwittingly change an already set outcome.

Except...from the worry in her expression and the urgency in her tone, he'd wager all was far from well.

His Adam's apple bounced hard in his throat, the words dry in his mouth. "Tell me" he wanted to ask, but said instead, "You're right to not say anything."

"I know." Her free hand twisted patterns in the air again. Her other hand curled inside his palm. "That whole stupid time continuum thing. It's dumb. What's the point of having knowledge if you can't do anything about it?" She dropped her arm to her side and tilted her face up to look him in the eye. "Well, I don't care. I'm going to save you Toren Limont. Don't think that I won't."

And for just one moment, regardless of the lack of innate magic he sensed flowing through her, he believed that she could.

Chapter Six

Aldreth paced in front of the large wall-spanning hearth, stepping through the dancing light and shadow the fire cast across the floor. Curse Toren Limont. Curse the entire Limont clan. Foolish, foolish pawns the Fae manipulated like pieces on a board.

Protectors of the balance of magic and mankind. Bah. A lie. Magic needed no balance.

Whirling, she faced the fire and froze, transfixed by the lapping spikes and flow that cradled birth and death in powerful heaving flames. Of all the elements, fire enslaved her. She rarely looked straight into the sparks as the blazing heat sifted away all thought and purpose, drawing her to its hypnotic spell like a hapless moth.

Her chest rose, cinching on a tight painful breath as images stirred within the tumultuous surge and ebbs, coalescing into phantom forms within the smoke curling away from bright conflagrations—sinewy wraiths of the past set loose.

As always, her grandsire stared back at her

through the hungry flickers, his blue eyes hard and penetrating as though he could see her, even though she knew he could not. He was not real, no longer alive. Death claimed him centuries ago. He and his magic with him. Aldreth flinched back even knowing 'twas nothing more than a spectral memory emblazoned upon her soul. A magical conjuring of an event every time she looked into flame, a lingering curse of the hated Fae, that all in her bloodline forever forced to remember the shame of Burnes Alduein.

In the fire, the apparition of her grandsire, Burnes, turned away. Chains of resplendent gold trapped his wrists, clinking along the crackle and hiss inside the large hearth. Slender ethereal Fae stood around him, light robes whipping about willowy frames in a harsh breeze. Whipping about within a riot of flames, sending sparks flying about the room.

One of the Fae dipped his staff toward Burnes.

"Ye have broken your trust."

The High Sorcerer lifted his head. "Ye dare speak of trust." Defiance curled the corner of his lip.

The oldest of the Fae leaned forward. An

ancient being, though he looked a tender boy of untested loins. The long slender hand coiled tightly around his staff in constrained fury. "Ye were the buffer between our realm and yours, endowed with gifts beyond all other mortals, yet you willfully violated your oaths. Had ye succeeded, our realm would be overrun with darkness."

"Dark magic that rightfully belongs to the Shadowrood. 'Twas trickery of the Fae these many centuries ago. Ye first thrust the darkness from your realm to the world of mortals, binding my clan as little more than a cork in the passage."

"Enough." The Fae slammed his staff upon the ground.

Burnes continued on. "Gifting an entire clan of magic to forge a bond strong enough between them to be the one bright hope of keeping the darkness at bay. The darkness that ye brought into our world. Ye have manipulated, tricked, and lied to us."

The Fae moved closer, the hem of his robe trailing behind like the spill of milk. "I said enough." His light hair flew upward, pulling back from his wide forehead. Aldreth gasped, helpless to look away though she'd witnessed this moment a thousand times before.

"Death." The end of another of the Fae's staff lowered to the ground.

"Banishment of the entire bloodline." Another staff tilted downward.

"The balance must be maintained else darkness return."

"A new bloodline will be established."

"One that holds true." The fifth staff lowered toward Burnes Alduein.

"One that holds true."

"One that holds true."

On a cry, Aldreth spun around and through force of will tore her gaze away, closing out the final scream of her grandsire as energy poured from the staffs to melt the High Sorcerer of Alduein in a crackling concussion of searing light.

They'd been wronged, she and her entire clan, forced to live as outcasts among mankind and the magically gifted. But the magic inside Aldreth had been strong. She did not let it die out, but instead sought wielders of dark magic and learned the ways to enhance what was innately hers. She had made pacts with demons, discovered their secrets.

She had become the most powerful witch this realm had ever known and with the darkness her life had been extended. Three hundred years she explored the earth and honed her craft, while the embers of retribution burned hot within her bosom. Her course was right and just. The Fae had wronged Burnes Alduein. They had wronged her.

She was the rightful heir, the last of Clan Alduein, bred to maintain the balance of magic in this world. Not the Limonts. The task should never have fallen to them. "Twas her burden, her right by birth alone.

So she'd gone to Crunfathy, disguised as a beggar woman, those many years ago. 'Twas a small task to unravel the spell of their defenses and coat the High Sorcerer's and his beloved wife's lips in poison. Took naught but one kiss between them. To this day, none knew she was the cause of their overlong illness and demise. She would have led the four young children to the same fate, yet…

When her gaze set upon the oldest child Toren, and felt the strength within him, she knew fate would see them rule together. He was destined to become one of the most powerful sorcerers the world had ever known. She felt the power within him, craved it. He was destined to be hers. So she had slipped quietly from the village to bide her time, to let him grow into a man, to allow his magic to mature. He had the blessing of the Fae. She came from the true bloodline.

Yet his stubbornness to even consider the possibility of a blending between them was maddening. He acted like a lapdog, too loyal and obedient to question his masters though the Fae kept the leash too short for Toren to see beyond to the limitlessness of how powerful their magic could be together. She had made a dreadful mistake. She should have taken him when he was but a child and molded him to her course. But the time was gone and passed for that now. She would have to make him understand. Albeit through harsher means.

His capture had been easy, almost disappointing. But with the aid of a demon, even a sorcerer as strong as he did not have a whisper of a chance.

She let her senses drift to Toren, deep in her dungeon constructed solely for him and smiled. He would soon be broken, pliant beneath her ruling.

She'd thought of him under her heels for years, savored this time she had of breaking him. She would be patient and enjoy it until she owned him, magic, body and soul. In every way, he would be hers. A delicious shiver passed through her.

She felt him breathing on the cold stone floor far below her in the dank dungeons. It wouldn't be long before he welcomed the softness of her bed, yearning for the difference. Yearning for her. She felt him drifting off to sleep so she let her essence follow the glowing lines of his dream to follow where his mind might escape to in slumber. She smiled at his tenacity. He'd thought to thwart her by finding a healer by traveling through time and now it appeared he meant to find comfort and solace in the dreamworld. Clever, clever, stubborn sorcerer. She would have to work on that as well. Soon he would come to understand that there was nowhere, through time or dreams that she couldn't find him.

Aldreth weaved her own spell to see the lines and angles of the trail he'd taken into the dreamworld. Brilliant azures and greens too bright and rich to look into for very long hummed around her. His magic was so vibrant and full. Powerful.

Heady. She followed him into the realm of sleeping.

He wandered his moor, tall and hale, a figure cut of the strength of the mountains attired in his snowy white shirt and plaids.

She coveted his power, aye. As High Sorcerer of Limont, Toren was the linchpin that held the magical balance of an entire clan, which in turn, held the balance of magic which flowed through the earth.

All that power, his for the taking if he would only reach forth and pluck it from his people. His people, Aldreth scowled, the pain of exclusion burrowing through her. *His people* adored Toren. He merely need ask and they'd fling every ounce of magic they had unspoiled into him like a magnificent vessel capable of holding the magic of hundreds of gifted.

There wasn't another sorcerer on earth who could take the balance of the world on his shoulders like Toren Limont. She'd waited for his ilk for a long time, for that strength of magic that should be hers.

So aye, she coveted the sorcerer's power, but she also desired the man.

He was hers.

A rustle echoed upon the air.

Aldreth looked to the side and her heart turned brittle. A young maid dashed across the moor, trailing mist behind her like gossamer threads.

The lines around Toren's mouth smoothed. Something indefinable darkened the hue of Toren's light eyes as he caught the maiden's hands within his. For that look alone, Aldreth wanted to plunge a dagger into the woman's heart.

So this was her?

His Healer Enchantress.

The one who had healed him and given him added hope and endurance to withstand her.

Toren kissed the tips of the maid's fingers and Aldreth's blood burned.

She could extinguish the lass where she stood.

Except…

The maiden could prove useful. Aldreth cared naught for the look of adoration upon Toren's handsome face, but she could use it against him. She did not desire his love nor adoration. She wanted to own him. She desired his obedience and fear and if his pining for this insignificant woman led him to that point...

Her heart sang, recognizing another pawn upon the board. Allowing him to have the lass and then taking her from him 'twould be one more reminder of how she ruled every aspect of his existence. There was not anything or anyone she could not take from him.

With a growing smile, Aldreth sank back into the shadows and watched.

Chapter Seven

C harity lifted one eyelid to peek around her living room. Nothing was happening. She lifted her palms higher and chanted out the Latin verse.

She'd been sitting cross-legged on her living room carpet, reciting the time-travel spell for a good twenty minutes and nothing had changed. As a healer, her gift wouldn't allow her to open a time rift and go back several centuries, nor could any sorcerer anymore even if she could find one who was willing to try it, but she should be able to manage a day. If Grandma could do it, she certainly could. Maybe she wasn't saying it right.

Leaning sideways toward the coffee table, she read the incantation in her grandmother's pink spell book again. No, she had the words right, even double-checked the pronunciation.

Charity shifted back into the lotus position and closed her eyes. Holding on a deep inhalation, she let her mind drift to Toren, which wasn't difficult since her thoughts had been filled with him since they'd met. She couldn't stop thinking about him, especially after their dream trail experience together. She exhaled and whispered the spell again with *Toren Toren Toren* as her focus. She settled the moment Toren first popped into her kitchen in her mind—concentrated on that as the spell's focal point. That was the moment she had to get back to. She needed to do this.

Energy crackled around her. She felt her hair lift off her shoulders and away from her face, caught in the current buzzing through her. The vibration intensified, curling around her stomach and tightening like a thick belt. She held fast to the thought of Toren, squeezing her eyes more tightly.

The Latin slipped around her tongue more rapidly, her voice slurring.

She felt a sudden wooziness. She swayed, pitched forward to step out. Step out? She was on her feet?

Charity snapped her eyes open. She stood in her kitchen. She wore shoes. Different clothes.

Oh my—

She'd done it. She'd traveled back a day. She was in the clothes she'd worn, the clothes she still hadn't washed Toren's blood out of yet. Her purse was in her hand, hovering over the counter where she was about to drop it. At least she wouldn't have to worry about running into her past self, since the way this particular spell worked, her consciousness simply reset itself into that moment of time, memories of the other timeline intact, and then she would simply start reliving life again from this point forward. It was the reason she had chosen that exact spell, so she would remember what happened the first time and could change it.

She gazed around the empty kitchen expectantly, excited to see Toren again in the flesh. Her pulse kicked into overdrive.

She set her purse down and...

The time rift ripped a hole in the air, shooting out churning winds that blew her hair back, and a naked bleeding sorcerer fell out of the chugging whirlpool.

And dropped to the linoleum.

Hey. She just mopped that floor. Charity shook her head. That had been her exact thought the first time she'd lived this moment. The reality of replaying this timeline and the memories of what had happened before overlapped in her brain.

Blinking, she frowned. She had to keep it together in order to do what she had come back to this point to do.

Her heart clenched, seeing him like this. Toren was covered in welts and wounds, blood and grime across his torso, hips and legs. His eyes remained closed though the thick lashes fluttered with each pain-filled breath. His wrists were torn and chafed from those dark bands that Aldreth had cuffed him with. The leather manacles that would pull him back.

Charity grabbed a stack of dish towels from her drawer and lowered beside him.

"Toren."

Dark lashes flashed open, glassy blue eyes focused on her, troubled and wary. Charity sighed. For him, this was the first time that they met. He wouldn't understand how she knew his name.

She lifted his head off the floor to get a few of the folded towels beneath him and then smoothed a lock of sweaty dark hair away from his cheek.

He flinched at the touch, and before she knew what hit her, Charity was rolled onto her back with two hundred pounds of disoriented naked

Highlander on top of her, pinning her wrist against the floor. Seriously? Again? Second time around she really should have anticipated that.

His gaze tracked around her kitchen, dark brows pulling down at the tall refrigerator before settling back on her.

"Are ye the Healer Enchantress?" he rasped and promptly passed out.

Oomph. Charity's lungs felt flattened.

Going through the nearly identical motions was weirder than that off-sense she got from moments of déjà vu. Like déjà vu multiplied by thousands.

She managed to wriggle out from beneath him—again—and get him rolled over. His arms flopped to his sides.

She pressed a dish towel to his worse wound and tapped his cheek. "Toren, Toren, wake up."

He looked so hurt and vulnerable. The urge to heal him as she'd done before threatened to consume her. She wanted to take every hurt away from him, but she couldn't. Not this time. Plus she already knew the extent of his injuries, the two broken ribs...

She also knew the depth of his magic. That's

what she had come back to this point for. His power and his sorcerer gifts. For what she had in mind it couldn't be wasted on a healing as much as that pained her.

"Toren." She rubbed his sternum. "Please wake up. We don't have much time." Only a few more minutes. The first time they'd met, she'd barely manhandled him into her tub and washed his hair before the witch Aldreth pulled him back to her dungeon.

But seeing him like this again, so hurt and in pain, was difficult. Charity wished she could take care of Toren again, heal him, get him clean, but the magic she needed superseded that. She wasn't even sure it would work even with all the reserves he had.

"Toren."

His eyes moved beneath his lids. His lips parted as he roused. Charity smoothed a hand along his cheek and smiled when his eyes finally fluttered open.

She didn't wait for him to focus fully on her. "I need you to listen to me. You came here seeking my aid and I'm going to give it to you."

His look of relief nearly shattered her resolve.

"But not just a small reprieve."

"Can you..." His throat worked. "I seek a healing."

Charity took his hand and squeezed it between hers. Jolts of magic passed between them, shooting straight to her heart. Gods, she couldn't do this, couldn't leave him in this state, couldn't let him go back to the witch like this. "I know." His plea had the power to unravel all her plans. What if this didn't work? Then she'd be sending him back still broken and wounded with little reserve to continue fighting Aldreth. And she needed him to fight. Just for a while longer.

She felt a tear slide onto her cheek. "I'm sorry. I can't."

His eyes widened, full of disbelief. "But I came—"

"I know. Believe me I know."

She didn't have time to wait. She placed her palm upon his filthy bloody chest.

The thrumming started in the pit of her belly, pulsing like the gong of a church signaling an old west hanging, drawing forth with the beat of her heart the innate magic that was hers by birth and heritage.

Magic flowed through her, tingling beneath her skin like static electricity. The tiny hairs along her arms stood on end. Focused, Charity anchored the magic within her heart and guided the power through her arms into her hands and outward.

Toren gasped. His back arched, neck stretched. Shoulders and head ground into the floor, but she kept going, kept pouring the healing into him, even knowing she caused him pain. Just a little bit. She couldn't heal him fully, so she held back while she let the power drill through him enough so that she could tap into his magic.

It was a dirty trick and she wasn't proud of what she was doing. It felt like a betrayal, but it was for his own good. It had to be.

What little healing she did on the way to his magical core was pathetically inadequate. The point was for her to be magically in contact with him so she latched onto his magic, keeping it within a stranglehold of her own.

And waited while the magic buzzed between them. She didn't push for any more, didn't delve down as deeply as before when their magic had exploded together and she had been thrust into his emotions and thoughts. She couldn't chance losing her focus or control this time. She just had to keep ahold of him—essence to essence—a light touch on the fringes.

"I need you to trust me."

Toren's glassy eyes barely remained on her. They flit incoherently about the room. When she'd healed him before, his innate magic had strengthened hers beyond what she could normally do. He had allowed it to flow through her freely and that emotional connection, almost a type of bond had been somehow forged between them.

Charity didn't know if it still remained or if the connection between them had been wiped clean as though it never existed because they were reliving this time once more. For Toren it never was. He had never been healed by her. This was the first time they met. Nor did he know her name.

Names hold power.

"Charity." She grabbed his large hand between hers. "My name is Charity." It was suddenly very important that he knew that.

He pulled his fingers from hers and looked away. "Is it no longer customary that a Healer Enchantress give aid to those in need?" His tone was an accusation.

She drew back as though she'd been slapped. "Of course it is."

A muscle in his jaw twitched. He turned back to face her. "Then why will ye not—?" His eyes hardened. "Ye're in league with her."

"With who? Aldreth?"

His entire frame stiffened, muscles bunching beneath his filthy skin. Oh crap. From his perspective, how else would she know the witch's name?

"I'm not in league with Aldreth."

Weak though he was, Toren scooted away, dragging himself backward on the linoleum. His features twisted with pain.

Charity crawled after him. "Stop that. You're hurting yourself. Your ribs have been broken."

Again he gave her a horrified look. Great. Sure. How could she know that? Like that wasn't suspicious.

He blew out the most incredulous sounding

huff she'd ever heard. "'Tis not what ye want? I'm at yer mercy, *Healer*. Do what ye will. I can feel your magic inside me. What do ye want? What is yer goal, witch?"

She grabbed his wrist. "Now you listen to me, Toren Limont. I only know about the witch Aldreth because you told me."

That's not poss—"

"Be quiet and listen."

"So ye intend to torture me with words?"

Charity dropped his wrist. Stubborn. She grinned. Bet he gave Aldreth just as difficult a time. Good. The thought of the witch and what she'd done to Toren made her shiver.

Charity got up quickly, keeping a tendril of magical touch flowing between them. They didn't have much more time. She needed to tell Toren what she had come back to this moment in time for, and although she couldn't heal him, she could give help in another way.

"Soup," she announced, grabbing the chenille throw off the back of her couch and draping it around Toren.

A dark eyebrow quirked up as he watched her

movements.

She grabbed a can of chicken noodle and shoved it under the electric can opener. Though trying to feign indifference, he stretched his neck, trying to see what was making the humming noise on the counter. Big bad torture device, also good for opening cans of soup.

Dumping the contents into a plastic bowl, she set it in the microwave. Toren's eyes widened. Charity leaned back against the counter to study him. If she squinted just right, she could barely make out a ripple in the air of the magical link she still had woven between them. She wasn't about to release it and so far he hadn't made any attempt to unravel it. Probably because he knew he could do so whenever he wanted. He'd undoubtedly already sensed the pathetic amount of her magical prowess and knew she wasn't any kind of match for his strength.

She smiled, trying to seem nonthreatening so he wouldn't feel the need to yank his magic away from her slight touch. That would be a disaster and so far, this wasn't going as planned anyway.

She took a deep breath. "We have minutes left

maybe, so just hear me out."

Toren's hands clenched. Great. He was being stubborn.

"We've done this before. Well, not exactly, this. I'm changing things even telling you this. Last time I healed you."

"Last time." Toren's eyes narrowed. So far so good. He at least seemed to take that in stride. "Ah. But ye will not do so now. Aldreth has gotten to you as she did all the Healer Enchantresses of my time so ye've traveled back to undo what ye have already done." He nodded as though fitting all the pieces together.

Charity's heart ached for him. "Is that why you traveled so far through time?"

Toren picked at the chenille blanket. "Aldreth threatened any healers and their kin who dared aid me. I hoped to find someone beyond her reach." He shrugged. "I was mistaken. Forgive me for whatever harm my rash action coming here has brought to ye and yer kin."

The microwave dinged and they both flinched. Flustered, Charity spun around to get the soup and a spoon, and then brought it to Toren, sitting on the floor next to him.

He eyed it and her warily.

She huffed. "It's just soup." She ate a spoonful herself and dipped the spoon back in. "I can't heal you, but I can at least give you some nourishment. Please. You'll need it. We don't have much longer."

His Adam's apple bobbed and Toren took the offered spoon, his hand closing over hers and that spike of energy charged through them, prickling along her flesh. They stared at each other across the plastic bowl of chicken noodle.

Toren let go and shifted back. "Mistress, I…"

"Don't. Toren, this has happened before. I healed you before and… " She fluttered her fingers in the air and he reached out and stopped her. Then jolted, his brows creasing together. Remembering? No. How could he remember something that for him never happened?

His eyes bore through her, examining, looking for the trap that lay somewhere within his suspicions.

The tiny lines between his eyebrows deepened. "Then why will ye not—"

Setting the bowl on the floor, Charity grabbed

his forearms. "Because I'm going to save you. Trust in that."

He shook his head. "Nay. How can ye? Aldreth, she—" He groaned. A tremor rolled through him and he flickered.

It was happening. Aldreth was pulling him back. The bands on his wrists were spelled to him, the glowing symbols keeping him a prisoner as securely as if they were tattooed upon his flesh. Though the bands were back in the dungeon, they were connected to him, still pulling him back.

"Open a rift," she screamed. "Now."

"Nay. I will not make it easy for her. If Aldreth wants me, she'll have to use all her magic to have me."

Defiant. Playing games with his captor. Holding out in every way he could. Admiration crowded the fear in her chest.

Charity clutched his arms more tightly as though touching him would keep him with her, even knowing it was his magic hers needed to stay in contact with. "You need to open a time rift. Forget about making it hard for Aldreth. I need you to open a rift for me."

Toren's muscles bunched beneath her hands. His arms shook. His jaw clenched tight, head thrown forward.

Time was out.

"Trust me. Toren. Please!"

He stared at her, understanding and horror at what she was suggesting dawning across his features. "Nay." His body started flickering, Aldreth's spell pulling her back.

"I'm not letting go."

Which might kill her since the bands weren't spelled to her. To prove she was serious she dug her fingers harder into his flesh.

He didn't respond. His head bobbed. Charity couldn't be certain if that was a nod or simply a jerk against pain.

She thrust her hand upon his chest again and followed the pathway she'd made down to the core of his magic and clamped on. And took some of it to herself for a better hold. Or at least tried to. He wasn't freely giving it to her this time, and there was no way she could get at it without his consent. A person's magic had to be freely given, not taken. It was one of the few built-in safety guards that existed among all magic.

All she could do was hold onto his.

"Please, Toren, trust me."

He was in so much pain, fighting her while also fighting the pull of Aldreth's link to him that was dragging him back. She could feel the depth of his agony in the tightening of his muscles, yet could do nothing about it. He'd come for her help and now she couldn't even give it in this. She had screwed up royally.

"Toren," she pled.

His eyes flashed to hers, intensely blue. He nodded. Charity didn't know what had changed his mind or if he was simply taking a risky chance upon her, but all at once his barrier came down and he no longer fought to keep her out.

Her magic grabbed a hold of his and drew upon it, feasting upon its strength and enhancing her own.

The air charged with static. Her bones vibrated with it. Her teeth hurt. This was happening. Now.

Bearing down against it, Charity lowered her head and began chanting.

She didn't have strong enough magic to travel

through centuries or open rifts into time and space, but he did. Toren did.

Just like when she had healed him, Charity tapped into his endless reserves and drew what she needed to her. What she needed to survive what was coming.

Images cascaded into her mind. The dungeon, Aldreth, beautiful in whorls of white. Toren, hanging from those bespelled bands against the wall, dirty and in so much distress, his pain assaulted her across the centuries.

"No." The Toren before her rasped. His hand circled her wrist tight enough to bruise though his flesh faded in and out. He would soon be gone.

"Trust me," she cried, and his eyes snapped to her, penetrating her soul as forcefully as the charged energy of the time spell weaving around them and magic poured into her, his magic, flowing as strongly as if Toren had dumped a pitcher of it over her head.

She nearly choked on the rush of it. And greedily took what he gave. Her grandmother's spell rolled off her tongue, a chant that matched the thunderous rhythm of her heartbeat. A short verse, really. She wasn't even sure if the spell was necessary. To her knowledge no one had ever attempted this before. It may not be possible. She repeated the spell over and over again, clutching at the words as hard as she clutched at the man's arms. The arms that were fading in and out beneath hers.

She was losing him.

Nooooooo.

Charity clawed onto his magic like it was a tangible thing.

Where he goes, I go. He needed to open a rift for her, but maybe he couldn't, maybe he'd used all of his strength just to get here.

And his hands locked around her wrists, solid and sure.

Air swirled around them. The curtains above the sink pulled from the wall, rod and all. Appliances flew off the counters, crashing against walls. Toren yanked her down as a chair sailed over their heads. Her little iron bistro table fell to its side and scraped across the linoleum, splattering the soup. Everything was spinning around them.

Her entire apartment had become the apex of

a hurricane, earthquake, and tornado. With them in its eye.

Toren's gaze locked hard onto hers. "Do not."

Too late. She was committed.

The ceiling pulled away into a black maelstrom of swirling, floating debris. Her kettle, block of kitchen knives, toaster, everything swept upward. Cupboard doors ripped off their hinges. The countertops groaned, tearing from their bases. Her sofa launched from the other room, banging against the wall, splintering the doorjamb.

Everything flew around them, sucked up through the ceiling.

He clenched his jaw and bore down. She felt it, the opening of a rift. It broke apart the world, splitting a jagged slash in her kitchen. It wasn't like the other time rift he opened. It wasn't like anything she'd ever heard of.

Charity was pulled from the floor and swept up into the roaring air. Toren's hold on her wrists yanked hard. She squeezed his arms. The flow of magic between them stretched and thinned. They swirled around and around until she couldn't distinguish anything. It was all just a tumbling nauseating blurred mass.

The electrified whirling atmosphere pulled at her. Scraped across her bones. Fillings seemed to loosen in her teeth. Volcanoes erupted. Lava buried mountains and rogue waves ravished shores. Charity's skin peeled from her muscles.

Her kitchen was gone. Her apartment was gone. The world was gone.

She screamed, but the cry was snatched away in the roaring storm. She clung to Toren even as the vortex tried to tear them apart. She shot her magic out to remain ahold of his. And missed. The tenacious hold ripped away.

Toren shouted, his mouth working though she'd never know what he said for all at once he was wrenched away and something hard slammed into her.

She dropped with a whoosh, forcing the breath from her lungs.

The air stilled in abrupt silence.

Everything was quiet. Except the ringing in her head. She thrust her magic out, looking for Toren. Nothing. She couldn't feel him, couldn't feel his magic. He was just gone.

Shaky, Charity lifted her head. She was sprawled stomach down in the dewy grass, as naked as the day she was born.

Chapter Eight

Charity sprang up. She faced a tall and impossibly wide stone-fitted wall. She couldn't even see how far it went to either side.

She glanced at the green forest behind her, and then looked up at the bottom underside of a balcony about thirty feet above. Or perhaps it was a jutting turret castle thing that was casting a shadow over her head. Had she made it? Was she in Toren's time then?

Her nerves jangled like the keys of a jailor.

"Toren," she shouted and stepped toward the wall—

And was thrown back onto her butt, her body prickling like she'd stuck a fork in an electrical outlet.

Ouch. Scrambling up to her knees, she reached forward and felt the pulsation graze her fingertips like an invisible barrier of crackling energy.

Not electricity. Magic. A spell.

That was the thing about witches. They were sort of like lesser sorcerers. They had a lot of the same abilities and could work a lot of the same type of magic, just not with the same amount of strength or *oomph* to it. Plus a witch's magic didn't just bubble out of her core like a healer's or sorcerer's did. A witch had to pull her magic out with the use of spells and potions and all sorts of magical objects. Yes, some witches even used wands as a focal object to call forth their magic and be able to focus it where they wanted it to go—as clichéd as that sounded.

Witches could also enhance the strength of their magic using spells and incantations to bind it with dark magic or even make deals with demons to become more powerful and more in control of being able to pull what is already inside them out from their core.

Because of this, witches—even good witches who never considered going dark side—had a bad reputation within the magical community.

The magical barrier buzzed across her palm.

No wonder Toren had been so roughly snatched away inside the weird time rift. This had to be Aldreth's castle with a spell around it to keep unwanted magic users out. While he'd been dragged back inside, the spell had repelled her.

Guess that explained the lack of guards around the area. Who needs soldiers when you have magical walls? Unless of course this was the back of the castle. There weren't any doors she could see. Maybe she could find some guards in the front.

Charity frowned, the realization of what she was up against rising to insurmountable odds. The spell Aldreth created just to make a barrier this size and constantly maintain had to be tremendous. Huge. She knew the witch was powerful. She'd have to be in order to conjure a spell on those bands strong enough to hold a sorcerer of Toren's potency. But an entire shield around her castle too?

Her heart squeezed and then seemed to drop to her toes. A cooling breeze shivered across her skin.

She was in the friggin thirteenth century, still unable to get to Toren and naked as a hairless weasel.

This wasn't exactly what she'd had in mind.

Her first priority: Clothes. She couldn't exactly expect a shopping mall to crop up. However, if there were guards near the front gates, supposing there were even gates...for all she knew this was like Rapunzel's magical tower with only one way in or out. She eyed the balcony above again. Naw, don't borrow trouble. There had to be gates where she'd find guards and somehow pinch a uniform or something.

Plan made, she darted across the tall meadow grass and into the surrounding tree line for cover. Safe in the shadows, she glanced back at the wall and walked straight into a tree.

A tree that grabbed her and rolled with her to the ground.

Why did this keep happening to her?

She was flat on her back squished beneath a long hard body. A curtain of black hair fell to one side of both their faces.

Hope blossomed in her chest. Had he somehow managed to remain out of the dungeon? "Toren?"

The long body stiffened. "Do not speak my brother's name, witch." The guy—obviously not Toren—pushed upward, balancing on his elbows over her. Grey eyes, not blue, glared down at her, but the features, even the scowl, was so similar to Toren's, this man could be his, well, brother.

"Col?" she guessed.

"Up here, lass." Another voice replied amicably and Charity's gaze snapped beyond the massive Highlander currently using her as a recliner and up into half a dozen more faces frowning down at her. She picked Col out easily as the fresh-faced tousle-haired youngest, who also bore an uncanny likeness to his eldest brother. Shapeshifter, the histories said of him, which made the scowling lug-not-in-any-hurry-to-get-off-her, Shaw.

Moon sifter. Whatever that was.

"Get off me." She shoved against him, well aware of how her breasts jiggled against his chest, and immediately stilled. Um. Perhaps he better stay right where he was for the moment.

Crap. She was in some deep trouble. Sure, she'd managed to piggy-back upon Toren's magic and get herself to his time, but she'd also been separated from him with no way into the castle dungeon where she'd thought she'd simply be able to get those spelled wristbands off him and they could escape the dungeon together. It shouldn't be too hard for her to figure out the spell and get them off because they weren't spelled to her magic like they were to Toren's. After that it'd be no problem for him to send her back to her own time and done would be done.

It had sounded so simple when she laid the plan out in her mind.

She'd been an idiot to think Aldreth wouldn't expect someone to try and get inside through magical means. The entire Limont Clan were the most powerful magic wielders of all time! Then again, she'd thought if her magic was connected to Toren's magic while they rode through time, she'd end up exactly where he was. Inside already.

How was she supposed to know? It's not like anyone had ever done this before.

"Let her up, Shaw," the young one said. "Can ye not see ye frightened her to shivering?"

Shaw grunted, still not budging an inch. His hip bone dug into her thigh. "She's shivering because we caught her performing a witch's ritual while skyclad."

"I am not—"

Shaw's large palm clamped over her mouth.

"Quiet you. We'll brook no foul spells coming forth from yer wicked lips."

Charity continued telling him that she was not a witch and exactly what he could do with his assumptions, although it came out as muffled gibberish which all the men ignored.

"I don't think that's the witch," one of the others said. He sported a perfectly clichéd Scottish red beard that could use a little one-on-one with a hedge trimmer, but he also had kind eyes and was immensely endearing since he at least seemed to be talking some sense.

Shaw rolled his eyes. "'Course it's not Aldreth. I do have eyes. But she's a witch nonetheless, working a spell out here for her mistress."

Charity argued that she wasn't a witch at all, *stupidhead*, against his hand, which of course came out muffled and useless and completely ignored. If she was a witch, he'd be a toad already.

"So, what do we do with her?" Col leaned his palms against the tip of a longbow.

Charity widened her eyes, more than a little interested in the answer to that question as well.

"Take her with us for now." Fluidly, Shaw was

on his feet, his hand removed from her mouth and was hauling her up in all her sheer naked glory on display.

"Wait!"

Before she knew what was what, Col's long plaid blanket thing was off his shoulder and wrapped around and around her, pinning her arms against her sides and a long cloth was shoved insider her mouth and tied behind her head seconds before Shaw bent and plowed his shoulder none too gently into her belly, lifting her off her feet and off they went, higher up into the forest.

Folded over his shoulder and without the use of her arms to brace herself, Charity swung with the rhythm of the big jerk's gait. Her cheek kept slapping his firmly muscled back, which she was sure made all the maidens around her swoon after him, but thudding against those muscles hurt. She felt lightheaded, her scalp tingling from her hair hanging down and all the blood rushing to her head.

They climbed up into the dense forest while she called them every name she could think of and some she made up, not that they could understand her beneath the gag, though she was certain at one particular savory curse, she felt Shaw's back ripple with quiet laughter.

She hated him the most. If he would've only taken ten seconds to hear her out she could have explained everything.

The Highlanders skirted a circle of large standing boulders, and then trudged through a stream. Freezing water splashed up at Charity's face. The forest and dirt and brush blurred around her. Her stomach hurt, jostled on stupid Shaw's shoulder and collarbone.

"I'm going to be sick," she shouted against the wadded material, but of course they couldn't understand her and nothing was done to ease her discomfort. Did these men never need to take a rest? Stop to pee? Anything?

Friggin robotrons.

Clenching her muscles against the nausea, Charity closed her eyes, hoping to ride it out. Although it really would serve Shaw right if she upchucked all down the back side of his exposed legs.

They ran on and on and when she was

dumped on the ground, it took her a moment to realize the world had stopped rocking.

Blinking, she looked around to get her bearings. She was alone in some kind of cave. Well, er, not a cave then, but some kind of small lean-to structure with long branches lashed together and curved into a type of dome and more piney bows making up the walls. Sunlight filtered in between the branches. Not exactly an airtight enclosure. Furs, blankets and satchel packs, even some axes and longbows were scattered about or leaning up against the leafy walls.

Ha! They shouldn't have left her alone near weapons.

Chapter Nine

Rolling to her side, Charity tried to figure out where the end of the plaid she was mummified within was so she could get her arms free. She gouged at the dirt with her heels while she squirmed side-to-side in an attempt to loosen the overly long cloth.

The blanket serving as a door lifted and Shaw ducked inside, paused and scowled at her. Col entered next, though his features lightened with a grin. "Ye look like a fish floundering on land, lass. Here, allow me to assist."

He crouched down and pulled her to a sitting position to begin working on the knot behind her head. "Be still, 'tis caught in yer hair."

"Col." Shaw growled like a worked-up watchdog. "Be careful. She's a witch."

The door-blanket-plaid-whatever was thrown aside once more.

"We'll soon know the right of that." Stooping to enter the low entrance was the most stunning woman Charity had ever seen. Thick auburn hair swayed around the thin yet curvy form. All that was needed was the soft gray gown to loosen and expose one shoulder for the woman to look like the heroine on the cover of a historic romance novel.

Col got the gag unknotted and pulled it roughly out. Charity jerked her head away from him. "I'm not a witch." She spit out fluff from the gag. "I'm Charity Greves from Seattle."

"Sea-at-all?" Col's nose scrunched up. Shaw merely shook his head, arms folded over his broad chest.

"'Course she's no witch." The cover model crouched before her, gown puffing up around her. Her lips pressed tight and her forehead wrinkled in thought. "Anyone can see that. She's a Healer Enchantress. A powerful one."

"Healer?" Col's brows shot up, disappearing beneath his overlong bangs.

Powerful? Charity restrained from snorting. The girl just proclaimed her not a witch, which the guys seemed to buy into, so she wasn't about to argue the point. But powerful? That was stretching it a bit.

"Ye're certain?" Shaw frowned.

The girl gave him a bland look that had the

perpetually angry warrior lifting his hands in a gesture of surrender.

Across Charity, Col and the girl shared matching grins. Both of their lips hitched up at one corner, popping out identical dimples.

Wait a minute. Siblings. The sister, what was her name? Irene, Deena or something. An empath. Just by proximity, she'd be able to feel if Charity's magic breathed of witchcraft or touched upon healing.

"Verra well, Edeen, she's not a witch." Shaw leaned over them all. "Then what was she doing traipsing about skyclad outside Aldreth's lair? And why was Toren's name the first to cross her lips?"

"Now *that* is a fair question." Edeen's brow arched just like Toren's had.

Three expectant faces turned toward Charity. She wiggled her arms inside the cumbersome plaid. "Get me out of this and I'll tell you. And for the record, I don't traipse."

Shaw leaned even closer, bending low over Col's head where the young man crouched next to her. "Ye'll tell us now."

Charity's pulse stormed to life. His glare alone

was brittle enough to crack windows.

"Ye best answer the question." Edeen folded her arms. Where she'd seemed to be on her side for all of half a minute before, it was clear that when it concerned her brother, Charity's welfare wouldn't be the priority.

"I healed Toren," she blurted out. Why not? She'd come to help Toren, and by extension, his family anyway.

The brothers and sister glanced at each other uncertainly, faces leaching of color.

Shaw recovered his composure first. Of course he did. "The witch brought ye in to heal Toren? She's hurt him that badly then?" Something changed in his eyes, like a flashlight beam suddenly flickering across a raw vulnerability that lay hidden far deep down. It tugged at something in Charity's belly. Seeing it was difficult so she looked to the others who wore their concern openly. Nope, that wasn't much better.

"No," she whispered, the tone resonating with the worry she'd glimpsed in the siblings. The last thing she wanted to do was cause them any more concern. "Toren came to me."

The dark veil in Shaw's eyes snapped back into place. "Our brother is imprisoned by the Alduein witch. He could not come to you."

Charity wiggled on her bottom. It was growing numb. She was tired of the defenseless position. Instead she jutted out her chin. "He traveled through a time rift. He said he searched for a healer who Aldreth couldn't threaten. He merely wanted a little reprieve so he could endure longer for his clan to get away."

The three went uncannily still, each with varying expressions of wariness.

"That sounds like something Toren would do." Col nodded. "Clever. Still imprisoned, yet he's thwarting Aldreth at every turn." He turned to Charity, one eye squinting as he asked, "Was he hurt bad?"

The question startled her. She swallowed. "Nothing fatal." She quickly went on at their pained looks to get it out, like pulling off a bandaide. "He appeared badly malnourished. His wrists are swollen and chafed where the spelled bands bite into his skin. The worst of it was two ribs broken and a few deep cuts. The witch is content to wear him down I think."

"Spelled bands?" Shaw ran a hand across his jaw. "Yet Toren got past them to open a rift?"

"He did." She nodded. "But for a short time only. They pulled him to the witch after I was able to barely help him."

"But ye healed him?" Edeen leaned forward and her hair spilled across her folded knees.

Charity frowned. "I…did, but then didn't."

"You didn't heal him?" Col's brows pulled together above startling green eyes.

"I did. The first time." As the trio studied her, Charity told them about how Toren had first come to her and she learned of the witch when she connected with him and healed him. She thought that was important for them to know if they were to trust her. She needed them to trust her. The shocked disbelief on their faces as she told the tale made her nervous. She really wished she had the use of her hands for emphasis.

She finished with how Toren was snatched back by Aldreth and how she had traveled back to that first moment they met, didn't heal him the second time, well, much, and hitched a ride through that crazy abnormal time rift on Toren's magic to end up at this point. Only outside of the witch's castle instead of inside with him. "So there you have it."

They just had to believe her.

Stunned silence coated the air. Edeen's eyelashes fluttered as though she couldn't quite grasp the truth of it.

Col's lips twisted. He opened his mouth to speak, but took a steadying inhalation instead and let it out in a rush. His hand strayed back across his dark unruly waves and he attempted to speak again. "That's quite the telling. Ye're from centuries beyond us?" Maybe they did believe her. He shook his head. "And ye believed ye could simply travel back here and pluck my brother out from under the grasp of the most fearsome witch of a hundred generations?"

It sounded stupid put like that. She shrugged since she couldn't lift her arms, which were getting sweaty within the thick plaid cloth, not that any of them cared.

"What about these leather bands on Toren's wrists?" Shaw said, then to Col: "Has to be how she's kept him imprisoned him this long."

"Aye," Col agreed. "If Aldreth's spelled them to his very person, getting Toren out won't be enough."

Shaw went very still, the kind of still of a predator before he gives chase. "We—" His throat worked and his strong features seemed to close up. "We take the clan to the standing stones."

Col and Edeen swirled to their feet, fluid motions of skirts and kilt entangling.

"What? No, Shaw," Edeen pled. "Leave Toren with that witch? She'll kill him."

"She won't kill him." Col's voice choked with sorrow. "Ye know that, Edeen. She's patient. She'll wear him down, break him before it comes to that."

"Even worse. Nay." Tears glistened in the girl's eyes. Col took his sister's hands between his. Charity's heart squeezed

Shaw stared down at her. "Had the *healer* not taken back her healing, we would have more time to figure out a proper rescue." His tone was bitter with contempt. "Toren will break. No mortal, even a sorcerer as strong as Toren, can stand for long against the Witch of Alduein. We'll break camp on the morrow and begin gathering the clan."

Without another look at her, Shaw bent and left beneath the doorway. Shoulders stooped, Edeen followed him out, calling after him while Col turned back, eyeing Charity with a strange look before he too left her alone in the makeshift hut.

Charity's breasts rose and fell with her breathing. *What had she done? What had she done?* She'd made things worse. Their whole clan was going to disappear just like in Lenore's book because of what she'd just told his family. It would have been better if she hadn't said anything, or if they hadn't found her…which…wait. What was Shaw's party doing near the castle?

Oh crap, they must have been on a type of recon mission, studying the lay of the land and the stone castle to make plans for a rescue attempt. But she had inadvertently gotten in the way of that. In the histories, the entire clan disappeared. Nothing more was known of them. Nor of what had become of Toren. She'd wanted to save him, but instead she'd taken away any hope that his family had of rescuing him.

Charity curled over on herself, shaking. She

never should have come because she'd singlehandedly just made things far, far worse.

Chapter Ten

Toren could barely lift his head. The last round with Aldreth's whip-master had taken more from him than he could say. His back burned, an inferno of ragged flesh that threatened to sweep him over the edge of the volcano from which he'd never return. He had to remain alert, had to focus his mind on something else before he became lost to pain and madness. He could not give in. Could never give in. He turned his thoughts to intelligent violet eyes and puzzling speech. She said she would save him, yet held back her healing gifts and threw herself into his hastily conjured rift instead. He didn't understand, just knew at that moment he couldn't let her perish from the spell of the bands pulling him back. So he'd oblique the Healer Enchantress, using the last of his reserves and now paid the price for it beneath Aldreth's lash and he did not even know why.

He could not really be certain that 'twas not all trickery, another ploy of Aldreth's to confuse him. Yet truth be confessed, he could not rid the maiden from his thoughts. There was something about her, something familiar, like awakening from a dream that he could not bring back to mind.

Charity. She had freely given her name, her true source of power. Yet she was clearly working for Aldreth or at least the witch had some sort of hold over her, otherwise she would have healed him. 'Twas a healer's creed to heal all she could.

"I'm going to save you Toren Limont. I need you to trust me."

Trust her? She'd pretended to begin to heal him and then sabotaged his magic and used it for her own purposes—whatever they may be—and then slipped through time on the strength of his power.

It made no sense. The flush of fever heated his skin where the cold grainy stone dug into the whip lashes upon his back where he hung against it from his wrists. Aldreth had been livid upon his return. Mayhap he'd imagined the entire happening? Mayhap he had not really circumvented the hold on the spelled bands, short time that it lasted, and traveled through time at all? Aye, and mayhap Aldreth had set her whip master upon him for no other reason than it pleased her.

Which it did. She had watched each stripe of the lash with rapt attention, a heady excitement flush upon her features. 'Twould not amaze him had she taken up the lash herself.

His sanity was slipping, no longer able to tell dreams from truth.

He must conserve his reserves, little that remained. Mayhap Shaw had already taken his family and clan to *Reolin Skene* and from there into the Shadowrood and they were beyond the witch's reach. If that were so, if there was some way for him to know with certainty that they were safe, then holding out against Aldreth would be a moot point and at least his soul would have peace as the witch stripped the last of his humanity from him.

If only he had a way of knowing they were gone, safely within the realm of the Fae.

I'm going to save you.

Toren pushed his head back against the wall.

Curse the healer and curse her soothing healer's voice. He did not want to think on her because her lie pulled to him. He ached to believe her. Believe that there was something to do that could spare him. Those dark violet eyes had been so convincing, he'd almost fallen prey to her lies. He had fallen prey. He'd brought her here to his time. He'd let his guards down and let her magic touch upon his. Her magic had been weak, insignificant, yet he'd felt...something. An allure, something so right and familiar about her he'd opened his magic to hers.

And what had she done with it?

Used him.

She rode his magic back to his time and abandoned him.

To scurry off to Aldreth and comply with her mistress's bidding.

'Twas fitting that healers were also called enchantresses.

They took a man's hope and belief only to stomp it into the ground like dust under her dainty traitorous feet.

Despair pressed into his heart.

Exhausted and shivering from fever, Toren let his head sink and tried to force the image of the beguiler's sweet face out of his thoughts.

Chapter Eleven

It took time and an inordinate amount of squirming and shifting into angles that would make her yoga instructor proud, but Charity managed to finally shimmy her arms free of the long plaid and after that the cloth was simple enough to get out of. Now to figure out how to wear it properly. The thing folded and wrapped in far too many lengths.

"Ye'll find these more to your liking." Edeen crouched through the doorway, carrying a bundle of dark wool and what she supposed passed for boots. Rough stitched leather with cross-lacings. "We seem to be of a like size."

Riiiight. If Charity had been blessed with something larger than a B cup.

"Uh, thank you." Grateful to have anything besides an overlong blanket, Charity lifted the coarse purple dress over her head and let the plaid drop around her ankles as the gown settled around her body. It was surprisingly comfortable and warm.

Tapping a finger at the side of her cheek, Edeen's brows furrowed. "Ye've put it on backwards. Let me help. Ye're really from centuries beyond, aren't you?"

"Yes. I told you."

Edeen helped her shift the gown around and cinch up the cross ties in the back, pulling the waist in form-flattering tight. "'Tis difficult to think of it."

They sat on the ground and Edeen showed her how to wear the long hose and lace up boots. Edeen's voice lowered. "The bands on Toren's wrists were covered in symbols, aye?"

Charity's fingers stilled on the boot laces.

Edeen's eyes flicked up and locked with hers. "Can ye recall them?"

"You're going after him, aren't you?"

Edeen glanced toward the short doorway and quickly nodded.

"Shaw doesn't know, does he?"

"He will never allow it."

"Why? Does he not care about his own brother?"

Hurt and temper flashed across Edeen's features. "He cares. If anything, he cares too deeply, but he understands our duty to the magic, our charge to never disrupt the balance. If Aldreth turns even one of us to her darkness, all is lost."

"Why?"

"Our magic, the magic of our clan, is shared. In times of great need, Clan Limont can come together and bolster our magic through our High Sorcerer especially, through Toren, yet also through any of our family, myself, Col, or Shaw. Should the witch or any other of dark power lay claim to that…"

"That combination of magic would be tremendous."

"Aye, and unbalanced. It cannot happen. If we cannot save Toren, we must cut him off from the clan."

"Toren would never—"

"He will fight her to the end of his sanity, he will, but magic cares naught if its keeper is in his right mind. The witch will win. Eventually." Her voice cracked. "She will corrupt my brother, though his mind and spirit will be destroyed in order for her to do so. We cannot blend our magic with a wielder who has consorted and taken from demonkind. Aldreth's magic will join with him and her evil taint will tilt the balance to a black stain. Ye have no notion of what that will unleash."

"Monsters." Charity's vocal chords felt raw, though her small plea silenced Edeen. "Vampires, werewolves, hobgoblins, ghouls, the dark Fae..."

Edeen's chest heaved in and out as though she'd been running. "We can't let that happen. All we can do is go into the Shadowrood before Toren's is touched by darkness. If his magic is unbalanced, 'twill filter into all our magic. Our clan has to leave and take our magic that once belonged to the Shadowrood with us to keep the world safe from the darkness. Safe from what we will all become. Otherwise...."

"Otherwise, your clan that is so strong together and meant to hold off the darkness will become the worse darkness. The taint will grow and fester and my century will be overrun with everything evil that exists with magic." She shivered. A thin layer of ice formed around her heart. History had already claimed the Limonts. Their clan had already gone into the Shadowrood, disappeared. And if they did not, the magical balance would be disrupted and evil would overcome light. Her time, her family, her sister—would be overrun in darkness.

The entire future from this point forward would be changed.

"Is there...?" Edeen drew back, her fingers pawed at the folds of her gown over her bent knees. "Is yer time bereft of magic?"

Charity frowned. "There's some, though mild. We sift what we can from the land."

"Earth magic." Edeen nodded. "'Tis good that some remains. So we succeed? We leave this world?"

She probably shouldn't tell her this what with messing around with fate and the Butterfly Effect, but who says she wasn't fated to spill the beans anyway? After all, Shaw and Col had been scouting Aldreth's place to rescue Toren when she'd popped in on them. Shaw had changed plans, making the decision to take the clan into the Shadowrood after she'd told him about the spelled bands. Who says she wasn't brought here for that very purpose? "Your clan vanishes. No one knows what happened. You and all your clan simply ceased to exist as far as history recounts."

Edeen nodded solemnly, though there was a tiny flutter of her fingers. "Then... mayhap Shaw is

124

right." Her eyes glistened with unshed tears. "We must leave Toren to his fate." Her eyes lifted, pleading. "Do yer histories reveal what happens to him?"

Charity could barely speak around the closing muscles in her throat. The woozy drop of blood pressure threatened to pull her under. "No. There's nothing."

Chapter Twelve

S ilence strained the air between them.

"Edeen, you and your brothers do what you must, go to the Shadowrood if you believe that's best, but I promised Toren I would save him." And she would. The image of Toren chained to that wall flushed angry heat through her body.

Charity shifted to stand, but Edeen pulled her back to the ground. The girl's fingers dug into her wrist.

"Ye do not know me, but do not believe that I would ever abandon any of my brothers without trying first to save them."

They stared at each other across the charged atmosphere. Charity nodded, her limbs heavy with relief. She didn't have to do this on her own and since she didn't know how to get back to Aldreth's castle after the trek through the forest dangling upside down from Shaw's shoulder, she couldn't do this on her own even if she wanted to. She had no idea where the dang castle was.

"Can ye recall the symbols?" Edeen's features had gone soft, pleading.

"Upon Toren's wrists?" Charity scraped her teeth across her bottom lip. "A little. This was in the center." She traced a spiral in the dirt floor and then added a jagged line shooting off its end. "It glowed. Do you know it? Will you be able to get the bands off of him?"

"That's Aldreth's mark, her family's symbol. 'Tis very old, very powerful. The mark of the High Sorcerer of Alduein. If 'tis that which binds my brother, he could not overcome it. 'Tis a wonder he was able to break free long enough to travel upon time. Do ye remember more? If I can see what combination the witch has spelled it with, I may be able to unravel the binding properties enough to get him free."

Charity's stomach dropped like a stone. "I'm sorry. I don't remember."

Forehead puckered, Edeen's lips pinched tight. "Mayhap I can help. I can guide you to the memory of it."

As an empath, sifting through memories should pose no challenge, but...Charity wasn't crazy about letting someone tiptoe freely around inside her head. She hadn't been too thrilled when she thought Toren had felt her emotions when she had felt his. It was just...personal. But if it's what it took... "Okay."

Edeen's eyes narrowed.

"Yes, I'll do it."

"Just like that?"

"Just like that. I've told you, I came here to help Toren."

Frowning, Edeen nodded and reached for her hand. When Charity stiffened, Edeen smiled. "'Twill not be painful."

"Okay, yeah. It's just—" She shook her hands. "It's a little weird."

She wasn't sure what she expected but the quiet nothing wasn't it. Edeen closed her eyes so Charity guessed she was meant to do the same.

And sat there, waiting...expectant.

She opened one eye to see if anything had changed. Edeen remained across from her, serene, breathing evenly, with her eyes still closed, thick lashes peaceful on her cheeks.

Charity closed her own eyes again and thought of Toren. She worried about him. Every moment she spent safe here in this stupid wigwam, he was suffering beneath Aldreth's hand—and she hadn't even healed him in this renewed timeline, given him the respite he'd traveled so far through time to receive.

He still suffered at this moment with broken ribs and with the way his body hung from his wrists it had to be excruciating.

Maybe she shouldn't have changed things, but rather left the original timeline alone.

An image of their first meeting flooded her mind, where she had healed him and something indefinable passed between them. Charity ached for that connection again, for his strength and compassion, even his vulnerability and fear of what might become of his people should he give in.

Once more she saw him as he'd been in the dungeon. Aldreth torturing him while he hung from the gray wall by the bands glowing at his wrists.

Charity started.

This was it. What she needed to see. Edeen had somehow guided her back to this memory. The girl's magical touch was so light, so subtle, she hadn't known the girl was present or was in fact prodding her to where she needed to go. Amazing talent.

All right then. Let's do this. Charity focused everything she had on the glowing bands. Her vision sharpened, seemed to zoom in on Toren's wrists. The veins at the inside of his wrist that she could see, pulsed blue. His skin was red and swollen. She looked at the thick leather bands, at the glowing forms.

Triangles with slashes. Crescent moons facing each other. She couldn't make out the other half of a squiggly line that curved around to the front, hidden next to the gray stone. They needed to see the rest of it.

Aldreth plunged a hand upon Toren's chest. He stiffened, screamed. Charity's sight jerked to his pained face, her heart swelling with compassion for him. Anger at the witch. This wasn't happening now, she reminded herself. It was only a memory. His memory that she had witnessed. She forced herself to look away and focus on the symbols. His wrist pulled against the band, twisted, veins bulging—

Charity fell forward. Her palms crushed the ground. Edeen had fallen beside her, her breathing labored. Her face seemed translucent, lips pale. She didn't look good at all.

Charity felt the girl's neck for her pulse.

The blanket that served as a door lifted. "I brought—get away from her!"

Crouching his way in, Col shoved a steaming bowl on the ground and lunged for them, pushing Charity aside. "What did you do?"

"Nothing," Charity squeaked.

Gone was the baby faced Highlander. In his place was an angry warrior focused entirely on her.

"Peace, Col." Edeen pulled herself up to lean heavily on her arms. "'Twas my doing. I sought answers through the lass's memories."

Col helped his sister up to lean against him, still keeping a wary eye on Charity, though his countenance softened considerably. "Ye should not have done it without I or Shaw near. Ye know how it weakens you."

Edeen let out a dainty little snort. "If Shaw knew what I'm about, he'd forbid it."

A dark brow rose. Were all the Limonts able to do that? "What are you about?"

Edeen twisted in his arms to better look up at

him. "Oh Col, I've seen the symbols Aldreth used. I can get them off Toren. I know I can. We can free him."

Charity narrowed her eyes. Had Edeen been able to see more of the symbols than she had or was the girl making a wild guess as to what the hidden parts of the markings were? As though sensing her thoughts—empath, she probably was—Edeen glanced at her, her mouth tightening.

Col looked stunned. Charity didn't know if he'd help them or be a hindrance by running off to tattle to Shaw. She was sure they'd get no cooperation from that quarter. She'd sized Shaw up as the kind who wouldn't budge when he believed he was doing the right thing. And he'd made it clear that putting the entire clan before Toren was the right thing.

Maybe it was. She couldn't really fault him. She just knew bone-deep that *her* right thing was saving Toren. She'd known that the first time she healed him and even though that blending of souls technically no longer existed since she'd reversed it by changing the timeline, she had felt it. Still felt it.

"Ye're sure?" Col asked Edeen.

She nodded.

Col stared at the leafy walls made of branches. If she searched hard enough Charity was sure she'd see the pistons of his mind rapid firing. "We'll need to slip out on my watch while Shaw and the others sleep."

Edeen's head bobbed and Charity bobbed her own head right along with her.

"We'll need a plan."

"I have a plan. Have had one a long time though Shaw would not hear it out." Edeen grinned, taking on her role of being the older of the two.

One of Col's eyes squinted. "Why does yer expression strike the fear of the gods to my heart?"

Chapter Thirteen

Col's watch turned out to be the last one before dawn. The light watch he called it. The easiest watch usually assigned to him since his older brothers still treated him as a child needful of protection rather than a protector in his own right. His stiff bearing spoke of just what he thought of that notion, the underlying rebelliousness evident in the toss of his head. Charity had the feeling that if Edeen hadn't broached the matter of them running off to save Toren, that Col would have done it on his own anyhow.

They slipped easily past the little group of slumbering Highlanders that had been with Col and Shaw when they'd first found her at the castle. They slept wrapped in their long blanket-like plaids around the dying embers. On an unconscious level, they were all probably accustomed to the thread of Col's boots during the early watch and to the light steps of Edeen as she preferred to wake before the men and perform her morning ablutions in private. Though a few of the men stirred, none fully awoke.

Soon the three were in the forest, walking in

silence while they made their way down slope toward the gray castle. By early afternoon, they came to the back of the stony fortress where Shaw and Col had first come upon Charity the previous day.

Col led them around to the front of the austere structure where there were, indeed, tall wooden gates and several guards stationed out front and two more up in the round towers to either side. There was also an adjoining stable where it looked as though many of the guards not stationed at the doors lingered.

Not that she could blame them. The castle seemed rather dank and foreboding. Who knew what they'd find inside. It reminded her of what she thought Sleeping Beauty's castle should look like, remote and surrounded by a dense forest. All it needed was giant thorns and the witch to turn into a dragon. Aldreth couldn't turn into a dragon, could she?

Charity frowned at the thought.

Keeping well back in the brush, Edeen revealed her plan and Col immediately began arguing.

"I do not like it."

"Do ye think I'm enamored with your part in it?" Edeen countered. "Ye have to grab the guard in the first place whilst I merely retrieve what we need from his mind."

"Ye're my sister. I do not want ye probing minds of strange men."

"For the love of—" Edeen threw her hands up. "Now ye sound like Shaw and Toren."

"In this 'tis well I do."

Edeen crossed her arms beneath her breasts. "'Tis not. And for the matter, I do not want my younger brother risking himself against the witch's guard."

"Hired mercenary I could take in my sleep. Do ye think that I cannot?"

"No," Edeen conceded, laying her palm on his arm. "I believe in your skill. As I request ye to believe in mine. 'Tis for Toren we do this."

Oh nicely played. Charity was impressed with how easily Edeen manipulated her sibling.

"Fine." Col pulled against Edeen's hand like a hare would pull at a snare. "But ye two stay put." He shifted into a patch of thicker brush and turned back, poking a finger at the air. "I mean it. Remain in this spot."

"We will," Charity and Edeen sang out in unison and then looked at each other.

"Will he be all right?" Charity asked, worry for the young man clamping around her chest.

"Col, aye. He's a crafty one. Been sneaking around, catching us all unawares since he was of the age his abilities came upon him. He favors sneaking in as a rat and then shifting suddenly into a bear or lion. Will likely more than not cause the poor guard to swoon."

About fifteen minutes later they heard rustling in the bushes. Edeen slid a slender knife from her belt, perfectly hidden along the leather, which Charity glanced at with a touch of envy. Why hadn't she been given a weapon to hide in her belt? Why hadn't she thought to ask for one? Because she didn't generally wander around Seattle armed. That's why.

Some kind of bird chirped and Edeen's posture relaxed. She shoved the knife back beneath her thick belt, out of sight.

Col lumbered into view with a guardsman

draped across his shoulders in a fireman's carry.

"Is he hurt?" Charity ran forward to assist in getting the guy off his shoulder.

Edeen stepped forward to help. "He's no good to us unconscious."

Col lowered the guy and situated the floppy arms along the man's sides. The guard looked to be in his late thirties with a wind-chapped complexion around a rough dirty blond beard. Old scars criss-crossed his hands.

Across the unconscious guard, Edeen gave Charity an I-told-you-so smirk. Then to Col, "Did anyone see you?"

"D'ye believe me daft? I nipped him when he stole away to fill the dung heap, if ye take my meaning."

"You can't probe his mind while he's out?" Charity studied the man's breathing, while holding his wrist and counting his pulse. The healer in her couldn't do less.

"Without being pulled into his dreams, nay." Edeen shook her head.

"'Tis too dangerous." Col slashed his hand through the air.

Edeen's lip twisted. "I need him awake and aware to differentiate between what's real and what are falsehoods of a dreaming mind."

"I can help with that." Charity smiled. Finally something she could do.

Col and Edeen both nodded and warmth swelled into Charity's belly at the tiny bit of trust thrown her way.

"Let me first." Col pulled thin twine from a crude pouch hanging from his belt and made quick work of tying the man's wrists together. "Go ahead."

Charity tried the direct approach first and tapped the guard's cheek. "Hey, wake up." His head rolled to the side.

Col's expression turned bland. "I could have done that."

Charity shrugged and this time placed her palm over the man's chest and concentrated on bringing the core of her magic up into her fingertips. She just needed a little burst of healing to buzz him with, just enough to refresh him and make his body feel well rested and energized. She and her sister boosted each other all the time during a harried day at the herbal shop, especially when Lenore had scheduled back-to-back massages with a long day on her feet. Worked better than a five-hour energy drink.

The magic coursed through her and—exploded. Magic ripped up her spine and into the back of her neck. The guard jerked beneath her hand like a man zapped with CPR paddles. He fell back and his eyes snapped open, bulging.

Col held him down. "What did ye do?"

"She's not accustomed to so much magic flowing through her." Edeen explained. "In her time, there is not a steady source of magic."

Col's head wrenched up, his forehead furrowed. Charity imagined what he must be thinking, the ramifications of little magic left in the world because of what his people were about to go through with.

"What are ye about? What's going on?" The guard thrashed against Col.

"I didn't know that would happen. Is he okay?" She'd thought piggy-backing on Toren's magic was intense, but this was, this was...like riding a thunder cloud pulling magic from the fabric woven in the air. And sun. And earth all together—and it flowed into her own core—into herself—she'd never felt anything like it. Imagine what she would be able to heal or cure with this kind of magical source in her own time? Cancer. Arthritis. Spinal injuries.

"He's fine," Edeen assured. "Startled is all." That made two of them. Edeen placed her palms upon the man's temples while Col held him steady.

The guy's eyes practically bugged out of his skull. "Stay away from me, witch. Get back." With his hands bound and occupied by Col, the mercenary started kicking.

Charity promptly sat on his legs and got bucked around while Edeen managed to stay perfectly still and focused.

The air hummed with the distinct vibration of magic being used.

Loose strands of Edeen's hair lifted like they were caught in static from a balloon.

The guard quieted. His face relaxed.

Edeen withdrew her hands from his head and smiled. "I have it."

That was quick. "Have what exactly?" Charity asked.

"The corridors we need to take to Toren's cage, the location of the keys, and where the postern door is. Would ye believe Aldreth's arrogance has her post only one guard where the kitchen help throws out the slop?" Her smile was dazzling and dangerous. "We can do this."

Charity grinned back. It was a crazy foolish plan with little chance of success, but coming here through time had been impossibly crazy as well.

"Déithe spare us all." Col's forehead crinkled.

They were going into the witch's lair.

Chapter Fourteen

Shaw slammed his dirk into the tree, forearm vibrating at the impact.

Toren was lost to them and that thought alone brought a pain to his chest so intense that he barely remained standing under the strain. He'd be cursed before he lost his younger siblings as well.

"'Tis as ye thought." Donnan scratched at his chin through his bright red beard. Though the thick warrior's magic was attuned to calling tumultuous storms, he bore the patience of a rock. Though even now clouds gathered above them so mayhap Donnan was not as peaceful beneath his surface as he seemed. "Their tracks lead off toward the witch's castle. We'll go after them in all haste."

Shaw nodded, the muscles of his throat clamping tight. He swallowed around them. "Take Hugh and Angus only. Go as far as the burn."

Donnan swung around, shock scrunching his wide features. "And if they've traveled past the burn? Ye do not mean to leave them."

Shaw yanked his blade free of the tree, leaving an ugly wound in the bark. "If they've gone beyond the stream, ye'll not reach them before the witch. They'll be beyond our reach."

"Then we'll *bluidy* well go in after them." The usually quiet warrior thundered like the storm summoner he was. In the distance, a bolt of lightning speared through the roiling clouds. "All of them. As we meant to do for Toren."

Shaw pinched the bridge of his nose between forefinger and thumb. He'd like nothing more. In truth, his blood burned to force his way into the gray castle and avenge the wrongs Aldreth had already inflicted upon Toren. The thought of his brother suffering under her hand—

Fury sang through Shaw's veins, stirring the latent magic always rumbling just beneath his skin. It would take the barest loosening of his control to let it flare out of him and destroy all those he held dear.

As a family, the Limonts were the tip of the sword that the world's magic between good and evil balanced upon. As an entire clan, they were the sword.

As a Moon Sifter, the only one born within five centuries that anyone was aware of, Shaw struggled hourly with his own internal balance, perpetually holding the overpowering force of his innate magic at bay.

No one, not even his siblings knew the strength of what flowed through him. He had never unleashed it fully for any to sense the tidal power within. He had never dared. It overpowered him.

Once Aldreth managed to turn Toren, what was left of the magic in this world would be overcome by darkness. Darkness would enshroud his people. There was no other possible outcome and he could not allow that to happen. A chill raced down Shaw's spine at the dire foreboding, yet even turning a sorcerer as powerful as Toren would be nothing should Aldreth discover what lay beneath Shaw's own dark surface.

Should Aldreth get her hands on his magic— he squeezed his eyes against the building headache—the force within him would do more than disrupt the balance. Far, far more.

"How would we free Toren?" he said to Donnan. His voice sounded as defeated as he felt. "The witch has spelled herself to him. My brother cannot use magic against her."

Donnan's face fell. "Mayhap the young lass and lad can find a way…?"

Shaw's heart pulled, worry and grief tearing at it with serrated teeth. The witch would take the younglings, use them to further break Toren.

"Go, Donnan. Go now and bring them back." Everything inside Shaw screamed to go after them himself, save the last of his family, but he locked his knees, steeled his heart.

Donnan nodded. "And you?"

Fists clenched hard at his sides, Shaw revolted at his next words. "I'm gathering the clan. Meet us at the standing stones."

The ruddy man's complexion went completely white. "Ye mean to take our people into the Shadowrood then? Take all our magic from the land?"

Shaw's heart turned to ice. He had no other choice. Once Toren turned, it would be the only way to keep darkness from devouring the world. The only way to keep the darkness of his own magic, moon magic, out of the witch's claws. Once she had access to Toren's magic, she'd have control over all their magic, the entire clan's. His. A lone tear slid along the side of his nose.

He hated himself. Hated the choices forced upon him. "We are the protectors."

Chapter Fifteen

You're sure this will work?" Charity paced from one tree to another, taking nervous glances at the brooding castle wall beyond the heavy vines and bushes they hid behind. The guardsman was trussed and gagged and stowed neatly beneath a prickly berry bush.

Col pulled his saffron shirt off over his head and handed it to his sister along with his stockings and boots, leaving him in nothing but the red and black tartan kilt sloped from waist to knobby knees. "'Twill be well, ye'll see. Just meet me at the postern door."

Grinning, he unhooked the pin holding the garment in place and without giving Charity warning to look away, unwrapped the material and let it drop. No worries or shyness about modesty there. "And bring my clothes."

Charity turned to offer him privacy as light erupted around Col. She twisted back, breath hitching in her chest. "Whoa."

"'Tis beautiful, is he not?" Edeen shone within

148

her brother's glow.

Col hummed with energy. The soft vibration rolled across Charity's skin. He was completely transparent, a human shaped form made up entirely of what could only be described as sparkling flitting fireflies. It was the most beautiful thing she had ever seen. Mesmerizing.

His form stirred, expanded outward like a heartbeat before pulling in on itself and shrinking, dwindling in brightness.

Charity blinked.

Col was gone.

She spun around, looking for him in animal form, her pulse revving up at his absence until Edeen lifted her palm and a tiny brown moth darted about her fingers.

"Go safely, *bràthair.*"

And the moth flew away. From the thick vegetation, they watched him fly toward the large gates, skim over one of the guard's shoulders and into the dark passageway where they could no longer keep an eye on him and know how he fared inside the witch's keep.

Charity didn't like it one bit. Granted she'd just

met the young man, but he had been the first one in this century to offer her any kindness or give her the benefit of the doubt. Plus, he was…she didn't know what…he was just Col and had already wormed his way into her affections. She didn't want to see him hurt or have to take such risks.

"Come along, then," Edeen said. "He'll be waiting."

Charity scooped Col's tartan off the ground and folded it while she caught up to Edeen. "You're worried."

Ahead, Edeen's back stiffened. "He's my younger brother. Of course I'm worried."

"He's never done anything like this before, has he?"

Edeen stopped to look at her over her shoulder. "When he shifts, there is a moment when Col is naught but magic."

Pure energy, Charity thought.

"'Twill be a simple matter for him to open the postern door, shift into that state and while he's magic, slide into the witch's foul barrier and push it aside to allow us through. Aldreth will never know he's there or that her spell has been tampered with.

His touch is light."

If it was as light as Edeen's had been in her head, Charity could well imagine that Aldreth wouldn't be able to sense it.

She'd gotten the gist of the plan when Col explained it the first time. In his energy form, he could penetrate a small part of Aldreth's spell that surrounded the castle easily. However he based all his plan on the hope that the witch wouldn't notice the disruption to her magic if he replaced the disruption with himself. In that moment of shifting from one form to another, Col was going to insert himself within that breach.

It sounded all well and good while focused on how to get Toren out, but now that Col was actually inside the castle alone, Charity worried over the young man. It would take only one thing to go wrong.

"Ye don't think Aldreth will sense him?" Edeen frowned. "'Tis such a small door." She realized the girl sought reassurance from her.

Charity forced a smile. "He'll be fine. You'll see. If it doesn't work, he can always turn into a bird and find another way out."

Edeen grinned wickedly. "Or a beetle and dig through the floor. 'Twould serve the lad right."

Charity grinned back, grasping onto the humor the same as Edeen to mask their worry.

They hurried to the back of the castle where no guards were stationed. As powerful a witch that Aldreth was, she had need of only a few mercenaries. The fewer men running about her keep, the easier to maintain control, Charity supposed. And keep from getting into the spells woven upon the castle.

An inconspicuous wooden door swung outward, disturbing several rodents that scurried away from the refuse piled at the threshold.

After hiding Col's clothes beneath a fat shrub, Charity and Edeen hurried across the grassy area where the thick vegetation ended.

They reached the wall and Charity looked up into the open doorway. White light flickered across it, expanding and shrinking at the edges. Energy hummed across her skin like a living force ready to snap at them. Aldreth's barrier. She couldn't see it, but she could feel it.

"Is that him?" Charity looked into the flickering

light.

Brow creased, Edeen glanced at her as though she were crazy. Yeah, dumb question. Of course that was Col.

What were they supposed to do now? His magical self—particles—stretched across their only entrance. Were they supposed to go through him?

Uh, apparently so.

Edeen gathered her skirt high, gingerly stepping between puddles of grease and moldering food remnants. This was undoubtedly the door whoever cleaned up the kitchens used to toss out the garbage.

She'd never again complain when her trash compactor jammed up or when the garbage trucks knocked over her big plastic trash can.

"Quickly. He can't hold this form long," Edeen hissed and ducked inside, right through her brother. She seemed to disperse in shooting rays of light.

Wow. Okay then.

Charity pulled her skirts up too. She could do this. Tucking her head down, she plowed in.

And felt...warm and safe. Playful, inquisitive. Emotions tingled through her bones and flesh.

Inside her soul. She never imagined Col's magical essence would be so infused with his personality. There was so much depth to him, strength and seriousness and deep-seated feelings overlaid with a lightness of being.

Then it was gone and she stumbled forward into Edeen's outstretched arms.

"Ye're through. Ye're through."

Charity grabbed the girl's arm to steady herself and turned quickly to see the brightness that was Col fade, only to materialize as a young man who pitched forward onto his face on the stone floor.

"Col." They both scurried to him, skirts puffing around his naked form.

"Col, Col." Edeen twisted his torso to get his head into her lap. "Col." She pushed dark strands of his wavy hair off his face and tapped his cheeks. "Col."

Charity found his pulse at his wrist rapid, but steady. Her palm splayed over his chest so she could monitor his breathing. She began to unleash a small tendril of reviving energy.

Edeen grabbed her hand and pulled it from Col's chest, and Charity's magic snapped back inside her like a rubber band. "Not in here. Aldreth will sense magic being used within her walls."

Charity nodded. Of course she would.

"And..." Edeen frowned. "I fear when we find Toren, he'll be in terrible shape. The desire to heal him will consume you."

"I can control myself."

"You say that but do not forget I experienced your memories." Edeen's features turned sorrowful. She looked away, her skin blushing. "I know what ye feel for him. I...I felt it. But I beg you, as much as ye'll want to, resist the desire to heal him. Not within the castle. We must get him safely out first."

"I won't put him, or us, in danger," Charity assured her, even knowing it was going to kill her to see Toren that way, really see him so hurt, not just through a memory. She ran through the list of what she'll healed before but were still injuries unfixed. Broken ribs, bruised kidney, several seeping wounds. Infection may have set in by now if Aldreth left him completely untreated.

Edeen nodded and turned her attention back to her brother. "Col." She shook him.

Dark brows pinched together into a grimace.

"Let's not be doing that again anytime soon."

Edeen's shoulders dropped in relief. "I…. Are ye well?"

Dark lashes lifted, revealing light smiling eyes. "Aye, well. Though 'twas not the enjoyable experience I'd hoped for."

Edeen pushed up on his shoulders roughly, though her eyes were soft. "I imagine not. Go on then, get yerself off the floor before we are discovered,"

"Oh, that." Col cocked his head to the side where another mercenary lay sprawled upon the stone floor. "He was guarding the door."

Edeen's forehead bunched in concern. "Did ye fight him? Are ye hurt?"

"Nay, but I could use his clothes." He shifted over the guard and began unstrapping the man's belt. "I bit his ankle, then changed into a man and clobbered him." His grin was pure male smugness.

He quickly donned the guard's breeches, blouse and boots. Col stood, wobbling a bit, though Charity kept a hold of him, suspecting he might be a little unsteady on his feet. He nodded at her in gratitude, not alerting Edeen to his weakened condition. No doubt his sister would hen-peck him into remaining here at the door.

"You okay to do this?" Charity whispered. As much as she didn't want to overtax the boy, she didn't want him out of her sight again either. They were so close to getting to Toren, it felt like an internal pull to reach him.

"Aye, fine." He went to the downed mercenary again, grabbed his leg and dragged him into a dark corner. "Edeen?"

"This way." Edeen took the corridor to the left, leading the way from the information she'd gleaned from the other mercenary's mind.

Glancing behind them, Charity hoped the man didn't rouse soon or that someone else came upon him like that in whatever those were that he was wearing. Some form of long underwear. Without any other rooms close to stash him in, there really wasn't any other choice but to leave him in the tight corridor.

Edeen led them unerringly through the tight passageways and pass the kitchen area. The entire castle felt like a giant maze, and they the rats. More so as they took several stairways descending deeper into the lower floors of the castle. Where else would a dungeon be, but in the dark underbelly? Charity thought dismally.

The castle was eerily empty. They only had to duck into an adjoining corridor once as two guardsmen walked past. Either Aldreth couldn't find good help or she wasn't fond of having too many people underfoot. Strange. Charity assumed all arch villains bent on world domination would want legions of minions around to fawn over them.

She shook her head. Her nerves were wound so tight her thoughts were loopy. Legions of minions. Geez.

"Shhhh, there's a guard inside." Edeen peered around the corner into a cave-like room where a lone man sat near a locked wooden door. The walls looked as though they'd been hewn out of the surrounding stone.

The guard sat near a small table spread with the remains of a partially eaten bowl of stew and a half loaf of bread.

"I'll distract him," Edeen whispered and turned to go.

Col grabbed her arm and mouthed "no."

Brows lowered, Edeen shrugged out of his grasp and sashayed boldly as she pleased into the dungeon.

The mercenary was on his feet in an instant, confusion stamped upon his swarthy features. "Ye cannot be in here. No one's allowed down here. Back up to the kitchens with you."

Smiling as though she hadn't a care in the world, Edeen moved beyond the guard, making him turn to keep his eye on her. She lifted her hand to his chest. Oh, geez, she was going to dive into his mind right now, right here. Except she wouldn't, not after she'd warned Charity about not using magic within the castle. No, Edeen simply had her hand on his chest, was distracting him...for what? Oh.

Both Charity and Col moved forward. Charity grabbed the pewter bowl from the table at the same time Col's arm lifted...and wham. She clocked the guard a good one on the back of his head. Stew splattered the wall. The guard crumpled to the floor.

Col and Edeen gaped at her momentarily. Col's arm was still mid-lift before he dropped it to his side. His mouth stretched into a wide grin. "Good whacking, lass."

The bowl dangled from Charity's fingers. She couldn't believe she'd just hit a man over the head. She'd never hit anyone in her life. Well, okay, maybe Randy Summerton in the third grade but he'd been picking on Lenore.

Not wasting any more time, Col dragged the man away from the door. "Keys?"

Charity's gaze snapped from the downed guard to that heavy door. Toren was just behind that plank of wood. She went suddenly cold, all her blood rushing to her toes.

Col slapped his palms against the door. "Where are the keys?"

Edeen searched the mercenary's body.

Snapping out of her daze, Charity sank beside her.

"I'll make him tell us," Edeen hissed, lips curling back.

"Or…" Charity slid a heavy iron ring as large as her fist from the guy's thick belt. A large skeleton key dangled. "We could use this."

Chapter Sixteen

He'd been hanging from the wall for eons. Time no longer held any meaning. Hours blurred into days. Days could be mere hours. He no longer had any sense to it. His entire existence pared down to remaining sane long enough to hold off Aldreth. *Nay. Nay. Nay.* As long as he could draw breath, it would be *nay.*

The word fell from his parched cracking lips like drops of water falling to the ground.

He could not be certain there was even a point anymore. Surely Shaw had taken their clan into the Shadowrood by now where darkness could no longer touch them.

Shaw knew what had to be done and would not shirk from that responsibility.

The door swung inward, grating on the rusty hinges.

Toren used what little strength he had to lift his chin and attempt to face the witch head on.

The Healer Enchantress walked in and his resolve plummeted. So his suspicions were correct.

She had been working with Aldreth all along.

'Twas a cruel turn of fate.

He let his head sink forward, no longer having the will to support it.

Truth be told, he had hoped to be wrong about her. He had started to seek out her image when Aldreth's tortures became too much. He would recall the firm determination to her lips when she proclaimed she would save him. Even though it was possibly a lie. He had been a fool, letting himself take hope and solace in her when it had all been another type of torture, a wicked game Aldreth and the Healer Enchantress contrived to get him to relax his guard.

"What has she done to you?" Her traitorous hand slipped onto his chest, warm and gentle, the other at his cheek, lifting his head so she could see into his face.

Lovely eyes peered up at him, brimming with convincing concern. He faltered, the desire to believe her worry was not false was overwhelming. His heart turned to ice caged within his ribcage. Nay. He would not be fooled again.

"He's feverish." *Edeen?*

Toren jerked against his bindings. His muscles went rigid. Nay, his sister could not be here. His gaze flicked to the side where Edeen's beautiful image wavered, hazy and indistinct where she stood close to him beside the treacherous healer.

"Nay," he rasped. "Please nay."

"Shhhh, it's going to be okay." The healer cupped his cheeks to keep his gaze locked on her. "I promise."

She promised.

His throat closed around a swelling knot.

She moved a little to the side, out of his view, her palms slipping from his face and gods help him, he felt bereft of her touch.

Strong arms slipped around him, calloused hands at his back, bringing renewed fire to his shredded flesh where the lash tore into him. He was pulled away from the cold wall and brought into a firm strong chest and he felt himself lifted, the weight of his hanging body taken from his arms. He cried out at the sudden ease of pressure as icicles prickled across the length of his limbs.

"Soft, you," Col's voice whispered close to his ear. "We have ye."

Col? A spasm rolled through Toren. 'Twas too much. They could not be here. They could not, but he was desperate to believe it. He let his forehead fall onto Col's shoulder. It felt so solid and real. His toes were lifted from off the stone as he was completely held aloft, the weight of his body no longer a burden on his overwrought arms.

"Can ye get the bands off or no?" Col's tone tipped with impatience, so like Col.

"I'm trying," Edeen muttered and Toren grinned despite that they were concoctions of his fevered mind.

Soft phrases, powerful spell words he couldn't quite focus on stirred around his skin, dizzying whispers of a fevered mind. Edeen's words floated like pale blue runes across his vision. The bands heated around his wrists, the telltale needling of a powerful spell being unwoven.

"'Tis not working," Edeen cried. Of course she could not unbind the spell. She was not real.

The heat intensified and all at once Toren's arms released from the wall and dropped. He cried out at the abrupt pain the sudden movement on his swollen arms caused.

"The bands are still on him." Col shifted him higher in his arms and his broken ribs and shredded back protested in agony too sharp to escape his throat. The lad bore the whole of his weight, which Toren thought was fairly impressive for a conjured imagining. "Aldreth will still retain a hold on him."

"At least we've got him off the wall."

"Worry about those later," the healer voiced. "Let's just get him out of here."

Apparently they were all in agreement for Col asked, "Are ye able to walk? Toren, are ye able to walk?"

Nay, he was certain he could not, though Toren nodded in the affirmative.

Col jostled him around to his side, drawing his stiff arm across his shoulders while he felt Col's other arm slide behind his back and grab onto the ragged tartan at hip. Toren's opposite arm lifted and a smaller softer shoulder nudged up into his armpit as the healer pressed her body to his side, cool hands against his heated chest and back as though she was ready to balance him whether he swayed forward or back.

"Oh no, his back," she cried and Toren could almost believe she cared.

And then they were moving and he realized how large of a lie he had told since his legs yielded no cooperation at all and his back was on fire, the bones of his ribcage rubbing painfully at every minute movement. A red-black haze lapped at the edges of the world, ready to take him back under.

The tops of his bare feet dragged across the uneven stone floor.

"Right, then." Col bent, dragging Toren down with him until his stomach hit the lad's shoulders and his feet lifted completely off the ground.

Toren cried out in anguish, his arms and legs dangling. Nausea rushed up to meet him but he couldn't hurl anything out past the crunching of his bones, splintering the ends of his ribs. He couldn't breathe around the gripping pain.

"Ye've hurt him worse," Edeen cried.

"Put him down. Let me heal him." *The little healer*, though all he could see of either lass were the bottom of their skirts swishing around Col's boots.

"Remember ye cannot. Not in here. The witch

will sense it." And Col started moving.

It was one of those jostling try-to-remain-conscious-under-a-horrific-amount-of-pain ordeals that Toren wasn't quite certain he could remain awake for. The dark floor blurred by with the slapping of boots on stone that echoed in and out of his awareness, growing blacker and redder with each shallow breath he tried to pull unsuccessfully into his lungs until the red flooded every surface and dragged him under.

Chapter Seventeen

Shaw felt the knowing gaze of the ethereal Fae bore into him like a carpenter's auger. Averting his own gaze, Shaw stared determinedly at the enormous stone carving, which resembled Gilfillon so strikingly, sharp nose, long sloping eyes, he may as well just turn to the lithe Fae's scrutiny.

Heartsick, he looked instead to the last remaining cluster of his people who awaited their turn to slip through the shimmery veil that led into the Shadowrood.

They hemmed around the luminous gateway, young and old alike, with their spines straight and stiff. Many clutched meager belongings or herded goats and sheep through the passage. Pride in his people streamed through his veins.

They had been prepared for this, knew it was a possibility once it became known the Witch of Alduein had taken their High Sorcerer.

A proud people, Clan Limont understood their duties to earth and magic and what would happen if dark magic overcame the clan with each of their unique gifts and traits, as a whole.

A small boy tugged on his mother's arm, cheeks wet with tears. "Nay, mam. I dinna want to go. I want to stay here."

Another ache bruised Shaw's heart. Aye, he was the leader who forced children from their homes and all that was familiar to them. He was supposed to be their protector, not this. Never this.

Gilfillan's long slim fingers curled over his shoulder. "Ye're choosing the right path. 'Tis a law of nature. All things eventually run their course. Even magics. Men's hearts are once again turning to greed and war. The time of greater magic within your world is at an end. Come little brother, relinquish your burden and be at peace." The Fae smiled gently, a boy's face with the depths of a wizened aged man's eyes. He nudged Shaw toward the glimmering gateway where less than a handful of his people remained. Donnan met his gaze, his features blotchy and resolved. The old warrior had returned with the younglings. He had not been able to reach Edeen and Col in time. They were gone, lost to him.

"Come, brother," Gilfillon's voice whispered like leaves floating on the wind.

But Gilfillon was not his brother. Shaw's heart shredded beneath a grief so profound his chest felt like a beast had clawed it open.

"Come." The Fae gestured.

"In a moment," Shaw snarled, his chest heaving, then more quietly: "In a moment. Give me time." This was right. Sending the clan to safety was right. He was never more sure of anything. But to leave his entire family…? And to the devices of a destructive, ruthless witch. He had saved his people, but *mo nighean*, at what price? Col's and Edeen's faces swam before his vision.

The Fae nodded, let his hand drop and looked out into the surrounding forest. "Ye have your moment. Treasure it well for we cannot risk leaving the gateway vulnerable to even the dark evil that will arise at the High Sorcerer's final turning and seek your people. The threat is too great. Once ye pass through the stones, Shaw Limont, we Elders will seal the Shadowrood forever closed."

Chapter Eighteen

Charity ran through the dark corridors alongside Col and Edeen. Across Col's shoulder, Toren's limbs swayed with each of the young warrior's running steps. She worried the harsh movement could force a broken rib to stab up into a lung. She'd healed his two broken ribs the first time, but hadn't healed him again when she'd traveled back a day and changed the timeline. So she knew the exact extent of his injuries. But there was also more. Sometime between then and now the witch had put him to the lash. His back was an enflamed mess of broken and sliced skin. He had to be in immense pain.

She nearly collided into them when Col suddenly stopped. They were at the postern door. The mercenary Col had knocked out still slumped unclothed in the shadowed corner, but something else, possibly the guard from the dungeon, had revived and raised an alarm. Shouts and footfalls echoed across the stone.

It was a sure bet that Aldreth would be testing

tendrils of any spells she had running in the castle. The spell for the magical barrier would be first as the witch searched for the slightest hitch in the invisible wall. Charity wondered how long it would take for Aldreth to test every strand of her spell-casting.

Crouching, Col pulled Toren from his shoulders and lowered him gently onto the floor where Edeen and Charity both held the unconscious man's head and shoulders off the stone.

"Ye'll have to drag him out." Col shoved the door open and immediately started to shift. His beautiful dazzling light form glowed even brighter within the corridors humid gloom. Expanding, the light floated into the doorway, sparking and sizzling where Col, as pure energy, must be touching and pushing against the weave of Aldreth's spell they couldn't see.

Col's light form stilled, flickering wildly. The effort expended to just hold the spell off a bit had to be enormous.

"Quickly." Getting her arms beneath Toren's shoulder, Edeen started dragging him.

Grateful he was unconscious so was spared

the agony dragging had to put on his injuries, Charity grabbed him from the other side and together they hauled him backwards across the floor.

Magic vibrated across Charity's back where she touched the barrier, thick and cold—almost painful, different from when they'd first entered this way. The presence and personality of Col was gone or far buried within Aldreth's spell, yet they pulled Toren in with them anyway. They didn't have much choice.

Sight and sound dispersed, buried beneath blinding pulsating humming light.

Charity stepped backward or tried to. She could still feel the weight of Toren dragging against her hands, could still sense Edeen beside her, yet they weren't moving.

Stuck. Trapped.

She screamed to keep going, but her voice was snatched away within the humming vibration.

If Aldreth didn't know where in the castle they were before, there was no way the witch wasn't aware of them now. It had to be her attempting to trap them within her spell.

She heaved back again, straining to bring Toren and Edeen with her. She would not give up. No way.

Suddenly Col was there, his presence like a candle flame warming her hand, somehow straining with her.

The white atmosphere groaned, shuddered and tilted like a box knocked to its side and all at once they were sliding, falling...

Charity, Toren, and Edeen slopped out of the door like sludge dripping from a sewer pipe.

They sprawled across the kitchen garbage and grassy weeds. Rats scurried away, squealing. Men shouted in the distance. Toren's head rolled to the side. His eyes opened and then squinted against the brightness of outdoors, though it was growing toward dusk.

Edeen rose up on her arms and screamed. "Col!"

His light form still stretched across the doorway was diminished and weak. The charged air crackled, spitting out wisps of sparks as Aldreth's spell closed in on Col and his light collapsed.

Col materialized, naked, light spitting and

sizzling around him. Slumping forward, he dropped to the ground.

"Col." Edeen lunged toward him. The shouting grew closer. Charity's head snapped up. They had to get out of here. She tapped Toren's face.

"Get up, get up."

His disoriented gaze tracked across the castle wall.

Slipping her hand behind his neck, she pulled his head up and shouted in his face. "Get up! Your family needs you."

His gaze finally landed on her, glassy and confused, though he nodded. The heat coming off his skin was tremendous. Charity pushed him upward, wincing at the tremor that rolled through him from simply getting in an upright seated position. She wished she had the time to heal him, even a little bit, but the guards were coming.

Toren pressed his arms around his stomach, practically holding his ribs together. She couldn't expect him to run, let alone remain on his feet.

Edeen wasn't making much more progress with Col. The young man was awake, pressing his hand to his head while Edeen coaxed him up.

A couple of guards came around the corner of the castle. Crap. Crap. Crap.

"On your feet. Now," Charity ground out. They hadn't gotten this far to let the guardsmen capture them.

Toren's lips twitched and head still hanging, he nodded, but at least one arm moved from his stomach to steady himself on the ground and push upward. His skin flushed a deep red.

"Now!" Charity helped as best she could, hauling him upward until he gained his feet and immediately listed sideways. Shoving herself against his side, she managed to keep him upright. Barely. "Move it Limont!"

She pulled him toward the tree line. It worried her a little that he went so complacently, a testament to how much pain he was likely in, but at least he was on his feet and moving.

She spared a glance to see how Edeen fared with Col, relieved that they too were heading for the cover of the forest. Edeen bent low, bringing Col with her to scoop up the pile of clothing they'd left beneath the bushes. Not taking the time to clothe him, she held the bundle to her chest, her other arm wrapped around her brother's waist as they hurried into the cover of the trees.

The mercenaries were coming, at least four of them she could see. More would soon join them as they shouted that they'd spotted them.

Their progress was difficult, made worse as Edeen guided them into the thicker areas of woods where sometimes the trees were so large and close, Charity lost sight of Col and Edeen altogether.

She also couldn't see any of the guards that had surely followed them into the forest. This was stupid. They'd never be able to lug the guys faster than the guards could chase after them. They had to stop, hide somewhere, so she could heal them.

Which meant she'd be sick and dizzy after a healing, but even so, one of the guys could cart her around a lot easier than she could either of them. Of course there was the very real possibility Toren just might leave her there. He thought she was working for Aldreth. Which…well, hurt. More than she'd thought it would when she considered the possibility that he wouldn't remember her or what they'd shared together. Of course he wouldn't. For him it had never happened.

Toren leaned heavily against her, his feet barely shuffling through the fallen leaves and pine needles. His head hung low, resting on hers, flopping slightly with each step, long hair hanging over his face. His breathing was heavy and wet sounding. Each little moan pierced her soul. How could anyone go on like this?

It was hard to tell if going into the darker part of the forest gave them an advantage or not. Sometimes it seemed the shouts of pursuit moved farther away, yet other times it sounded as though the guardsmen were suddenly right upon them and Charity's heart sped up.

Col seemed to rouse a bit, walking steadier. Sometime along the way, he'd managed to wrap his kilt around his waist, or maybe Edeen had done it for him.

"We need to stop. Toren can't keep going like this," she called to Edeen when they came near enough.

"In here." Edeen took them into a dried-up stream bed and beneath a jumble of slender fallen trees and long branches that looked like a fast moving stream had carried the debris all to a point where they caught against rocks jammed together. There was just enough room to hunker down inside.

They got the men situated. Once Col hit the ground, it appeared all the reserves he'd utilized to get this far left him and he promptly passed out.

Just perfect.

Toren moaned, curling over to his side to ease the pressure on his ribs. His sweaty hair was plastered to his scalp and face. There was a bit of blood at his bluing lips. One or both of his ribs must have pierced something internally. His breathing was harsh and ragged, but at least he was still breathing. Whatever the damage, it couldn't be left any longer. She had to heal him now.

Charity pushed the damp hair from his cheek and Toren flinched. "Nay." His plea was a breathy rasp.

Her heart clenching, Charity let her hand drop in exhaustion.

Edeen's hand feathered over her arm. "'Tis the fever."

"I guess I should be happy he let me help him

as much as he did. He thinks I'm in cahoots with Aldreth. Like I'd have anything to do with that witch." They didn't have time for his delusions about her.

"I…" Edeen's shoulders hunched with exhaustion. "He's out of his head but 'twill be all right. We have him now." Her arms swung around Charity and she pressed her head into her shoulder. "Thank you for coming. Thank you for helping us get my brother out." The ends of her hair swayed as she shook her head. "I felt the depth of your connection—yours and Toren's. I know what you did. I know you gave up his memories of you to travel beyond yer past. Charity, 'twas a brave thing to do. I wish…" Edeen didn't finish. Her hands went to one of the bands still upon Toren's wrists. "We need to get these off. As long as he wears them, Aldreth can find him and any magic he possesses is useless against her."

Healing first. She didn't like the ashy tone to his skin or the sound of his breathing. "I don't suppose we can just cut them off?"

Edeen shook her head. "'Tis a powerful spell. I tried, but could not unravel it fully."

Charity pushed a lock of Edeen's hair behind her ear, a gesture she often made with Lenore. "You did enough to get him out."

"But will it be enough?" Unshed tears glistened in the girl's eyes. She pulled on the bands. "Aldreth has the means to find him and take him back at will."

Charity stopped her before she did more damage to the torn flesh beneath the leather. The symbols carved into them glowed at her touch.

Both girls stilled, watching to see if they would light up again. That couldn't be good.

"It will be all right," Charity assured. "We didn't come this far to fail. Aldreth will have to go through me to get at Toren."

"Aye." Edeen's lip fell into a thin line. "Through me as well."

They shared a grim smile.

Charity shuffled closer to Toren. "I'm going to do what I can to heal him."

"Ye're exhausted," Edeen protested.

"I'll be more exhausted if I have to keep lugging half of his weight. Besides, I don't think it can be put off." He was so pale, his features scrunched tight in pain. "I have to do this now." She glanced at Col, softly snoring on the other side of Toren. "Toren's hurt pretty bad. I' don't think I'll have enough energy for Col as well."

Edeen nodded. "Do what you must for Toren. Col is merely weakened from remaining in his magical form overlong. He should recover on his own." Edeen stroked the young man's cheek. "I'm sure of it." Her tone didn't exactly convey the same certainty. "Remain here with them and do what you can. I'm going to go cover our tracks."

Charity nodded, already placing her palm upon Toren's blood-caked chest and gathered her magic from far within her core. "Please be careful."

Edeen nodded and slipped away.

Chapter Nineteen

*A*ldreth will have to go through me to get at
Toren.

Her voice fluttered around his consciousness
like ribbons of silk. He'd sensed that conviction
earlier. *I will save you.*

Toren panted around the sharpness in his side,
his breaths too shallow to fully expand his
burdened lungs. He was at once excruciatingly hot
then brutally cold. Long shivers seized muscles that
brought more pain, more torture. His back was an
inferno.

He swam against the current in a sea of
delirium, uncomprehending of what was truly real.

Aldreth had won. Madness had taken him and
now she would be able to take his magic as easily
as plucking an egg from a nest.

He couldn't think, could do naught but tense
his body, clench uncooperative muscles to stave off
the burning agony that was his flesh. To make it
stop, to climb out of this pit, he would promise her
anything. Nay, he could not give in. He must
endure, let it consume him.

"Toren, I'm going to fix this." The soothing voice crooned across his forehead like a caress, puffs of cooling breath close to his hot skin. 'Twas Aldreth's healer, she of the ebony tresses and piercing violet eyes. She ran to him through the mists, concern weighing down delicate brows. The slight pressure of her palm rested upon his sternum.

I'm going to save you Toren Limont. Don't think I won't.

He so wanted to believe her. But it had never happened. She was naught but a lie.

Toren rolled his head back and forth, cradled within a feminine lap. That had never happened either, though the scene rippled through his emotions like a lost memory.

I need your name.

Her words whispered over his heated skin.

And he had given it, trusted her with his name like offering a precious pearl.

When? When had he done that? He couldn't remember. Images overlaid upon another. He was in her strange home. She refused to heal him. Nay, she did heal him. His head rolled again. His arms flailed as he reached out…for what?

Nothing made sense. Darkness clouded his mind, the black wing of a vulture blotting out the sun.

Heat scalded his lungs. Burning. From inside. And without. His back was on fire. He burned, he burned. He was on fire for nothing else could explain the flames.

His ribs moved. He cried out within the tide of brutality, recognizing the vicious force demanded of a healing. Someone was trying to heal him. Or hurt him worse. He did not know.

He rolled to get away from it, unsure that he'd survive what was happening, yet an arm flew around his waist, holding him in place and a voice wept close to his cheek.

"I'm sorry. I'm sorry. It will be better soon. I promise."

He settled for her, riding it through, for he hadn't the strength to do aught else and found that the inferno was fading, cooling. He could breathe, the blockage in his lungs was no longer present. Harsh breaths expanded his chest in and out until he found his breathing slowed of its own accord, following another's pattern.

"In. Out. In. Out. That's good. Breathe with me. In and out. You're doing good."

His eyes fluttered open to lips that stretched into a smile. Lips that were above him and very close to his own.

"Toren?"

He shoved away from her, half-surprised he could do so without more than a dull ache. Still weak, his arms buckled, threatening to pitch him forward.

The healer, too, supported herself with shaky arms, also weakened from the healing, yet 'twas the crestfallen look of disbelief that made him want to rush back to her side. Nay, he could not afford to be tricked again.

He pressed the flat of his palm to his head as though he could push hard enough and reorder his jumbled thoughts.

He had no recollection of what had transpired or if what he did remember was actually truth. His thoughts were a muddled mess.

They were inside a tangle of tree limbs and mud. Col lay unconscious beside him in the muck and the world took a dizzying spin around him.

He shook his head to right the world back in place, surprised when no pain assailed him at the movement. "What have ye done to my brother?"

"I—" If anything the healer looked hurt, her incredible eyes widened. "I didn't do anything." She shifted toward them.

Toren threw out his hand. "Stay back. Just stay right there. I'm taking my brother out of here."

"What? Are you kidding me?" Now she appeared indignant.

"Nay. I am not *kidding* ye." He didn't like how unnaturally still Col was. Keeping an eye on the healer, he sidled over to his brother. "Col." He nudged his shoulder and the lad's eyes stirred beneath his lids. If the healer had harmed him…

Edging out of the enclosure backwards, Toren grabbed Col's arm and the fabric at his hip and pulled him across the soft squishy ground.

The Healer Enchantress slammed her fists on her hips. Even on her knees and tiny as she was, she looked like a woman not to be trifled with.

"What are you doing? Where do you think you're taking him?"

To his home. Someone in the clan would know how to undo whatever she had done to him. Except... He squinted through disordered memories, unable to think clearly. That wasn't right. He couldn't take Col back to the village because the clan had left. Surely they had gone to *Reolin Skene* by now.

He had to take Col there. Hopefully they weren't too late, but if they were, he would call on the Fae to open the gateway and get his brother to the safety of the Shadowrood. He expected that the Fae could also somehow rid him of these spelled bands. And then once his entire clan was safe, he would come back for Aldreth. She could no longer be free to wreak havoc on the world, with or without his clan already gone.

When he was finished with the witch, he'd find a special punishment for the little healer. An image of creamy skin and pliant curves beneath him in an altogether different form of punishment came unbidden to his thoughts and all the blood rushed from his head. *Déithe.* He shook it off. *Enchantress,* he glared at her.

He found Col's saffron shirt and also his boots

next to him and began clothing his brother, tugging the shaggy head through the fabric and guiding the limp arms through the sleeves.

"Fine," the healer huffed. "I'm the bad guy. What of your sister then?"

Toren went rigid, recalling his sister's voice had been floating at the edge of his delirium. Did the witch have her?

"What have ye done with her?"

"Now you're just being stupid." The healer crossed her arms beneath her breasts and Toren's traitorous eyes couldn't help following the movement down from her face. She was breathing hard, thought trying to hide it, shaking and pale, at the end of her endurance after healing him. Which...why had she bothered to heal him?

Those violet eyes sparked with temper. "All by myself, I overpowered a shapeshifter, an extraordinarily gifted empath, *and* carried your heavy sorry ass all over this godforsaken forest. For what purpose? Oh yeah, and then I healed you. Let's not forget that. If I'm working with Aldreth, wouldn't it have been easier to leave you all in the dungeon once I lured Col and Edeen there? Three

Limonts for the price of one. Sheesh. This is really insulting, you know that?"

Her eye's sparked. They were far too expressive. He could fair see every emotion flit across her lovely face, though he was not prepared to stomp caution to the ground as long as Col and Edeen were at risk.

He frowned, his head so muggy with clashing images and conflicting emotions toward the woman, he didn't know what to make of her. One moment he wanted to throttle her while the next he felt the overwhelming need to scoop her into his arms and kiss the scowl he'd put there off of her brow. As it was, she was little threat right now in her weakened condition. Right now, Col was his main concern.

"She makes a valid point, Toren." Edeen crawled beneath the tangled branches.

Toren's gaze whipped to her, relief clenching tight in his stomach. Before he realized he'd covered the small distance, even with the aches in his body, he had her crushed against him. He hadn't dared believe he'd see any of his family again, but here Edeen was, hale and free and he was determined to keep her and Col that way.

Déithe, what was she doing here? She and Col should have gone into the Shadowrood by now.

Edeen clung just as tightly to him, her slender hands clutching tight to the skin of his back—his back that was no longer a mass of shredded meat thanks to the healer— unwilling to let go when he eased Edeen away to look her over. She was disheveled, the hem of her kirtle encrusted with dirt, but otherwise appeared unscathed, a beautiful sight to his tortured soul.

Behind him came the thump of a body hitting the ground.

Edeen's features went from relief to concern and she was out of his arms and moving in a flash of flying skirts.

Toren turned to find the little healer unconscious on the ground.

For a moment all he could do was stare. Conflicting feelings roiled through him. She looked so fragile, dark hair spilled over the ground. Thick lashes formed half-circles upon her pale cheeks.

He crouched, scooping her into his arms before he realized he had even moved.

Beside them, Edeen smoothed a lock of hair off Charity's forehead. "Healing you has left her exhausted." She frowned at him. "Yer injuries were...Oh Toren, the witch hurt you so. How you suffered..."

Toren frowned. He had been angry, confused. He still didn't know what to think of her or her part in his torture or rescue, but he couldn't think beyond the fact that she had taxed herself for him and he wanted her to wake up.

"What's happened?" He knew he would get the truth of events from Edeen.

"We've freed you, Toren. We got you out."

"Aye." That much was obvious. His gaze slanted to the healer, desiring to see those sparking violet eyes open. "But how? And what ails Col?"

Worry lines puckered Edeen's forehead and she shook her head and reached over to take Col's hand on her other side. "He pushed into Aldreth's barriers while in the state between shifting." Edeen winced up at him. "'Twas the only way to get to you."

Toren went cold. 'Twas dangerous for a shifter to hold that state of magic overlong. Many had tried and been lost—simply dissipating into the ether. And to do so within a witch's spell... *Déithe* A shudder rolled through his frame. How long had Col maintained that form? 'Twas a testament to his brother's ability...or his desperation.

Toren looked at Col, his gut twisting in fear, yet Col was solid and alive, his chest softly rising and falling. He could so easily lost him and never known of it while languishing deep in Aldreth's dungeon.

Tamping down the panic filling in his chest, Toren stroked the healer's arm before he realized what he was doing. He didn't stop. "What part has she played in all this?"

He regretted the harsh tone at the widening of Edeen's eyes and the way her features conveyed precisely how much his distrust of the healer annoyed her. His resolve nearly faltered.

"Charity." Edeen's chin set in a stubborn tilt. "She has a name so ye best use it. 'Twas she who brought us the descriptions of the symbols at your wrists and allowed me to unravel Aldreth's spell." She faltered when he glanced at one of the bands. "Partially unraveled. Enough to get ye away from the castle."

He knew the healer's name for rood's sake. He just couldn't think of her in so familiar a term if he were to keep from falling prey to her bewitchment. Enchantress was an apt description of the healers. He had the discomfiting feeling that If Aldreth would have thrown this lass to him, he would have succumbed long ago.

He hesitated, looking from the still woman who felt so right in his arms to his sister and then to Col, the instinct to protect his siblings from anything— anything at all—ingrained into his very existence. Col's utter stillness unnerved him.

"She healed you." Edeen's palm curled over his arm, her gaze penetrating. "I trust her."

And just that easily Toren's hard-waged battle was lost. *Empath*. He'd been under Aldreth's ministrations so long that he dare not trust his own feelings, but he could trust Edeen's.

A peace he had not felt for sennights settled around him and he nodded. Edeen trusted this woman. So would he, though he was not prepared for the sudden twist in his heart or the tightness in his throat over the decision as he stared down at her, memorizing every feature. He pushed away the urge to plunge his fingers into her hair.

They needed to go. He did not have the full details of his rescue, but he could not imagine that Aldreth would not soon be upon them. "How many have followed us?" Whether the witch had sent men after them or not was not in question.

"'Tis difficult to tell within the forest. Nine by my reckoning."

Only nine? "Aldreth is holding them back. I'm certain they know exactly where we are."

Edeen's face paled. Her gaze lowered to the bands of leather on his wrist. "Why would she hold them back? For what purpose?"

"Purpose?" Toren barked out a harsh laugh. "She plays with us. She has no need of mercenaries to track us through the forest." He lifted his wrist. The symbols glowed slightly beneath the tangled branches. "She can pull me back at will."

Col stirred. His eyes moved beneath his eyelids.

"Then why?" Edeen stared down at Col, the lines of her forehead smoothed as she made the connection. "For us. Col and I. Aldreth means to follow her connection to you and find us all together."

As though hearing his name spoken, Col's lashes lifted, revealing mossy green eyes. His lips twitched into a smile. "Did it work?" Relief eased the worry straining Toren's chest.

"Aye, it worked, ye mutton head." Edeen ruffled the lad's hair. "D'ye not recall walking through the forest?"

Col's brow wrinkled and he grimaced. "Unnn. I do not recall much after carrying Toren through the passages."

"I would think not." Edeen pushed Col's hair from his cheek. "Can you walk?"

"Of course. What of Toren?"

"Of my own volition, brother."

Col's eyes swept to him and the young warrior's entire countenance lifted in what Toren could only describe as unreserved joy. "Toren." He pulled up, his gaze immediately falling upon the healer. "What's happened to Charity?"

Protectiveness swelled inside Toren's chest. *She ran to him, across the moor, mist curling at her hips, teasing cloudy swirls around her breech-*

covered legs until she stood before him, slender hands upon his crisp white shirt.

"Toren," she breathed.

He smiled at the unusual inflection she gave to his name and since she was but a dream, he indulgently dragged his fingers into her hair, sighing at the silkiness.

"Toren, I need you to tell me where you are. I'm going to help you."

He stared down at her, could not tear his gaze away.

"Imigh sa diabhal, Toren," Col muttered, snapping Toren back from the memory. Was it a memory? "How could ye let the witch get the advantage over you?"

How indeed. His abduction was all a bit fuzzy. There'd been a lovely wench, nay, not a wench after all. He had glimpsed her true form—a demon—and before he knew it the cursed wrist bands were on him and Aldreth appeared. None of his magic could be called against her where hers worked magnificently well against him.

"'Tis a tale for another time." Though humiliating, he would not have any others of his clan fall to the same fate. "Let's get ye up."

Col pulled back, his demeanor turned serious. "Do not do so again."

Toren grinned at the warning. "Nay."

"Is the way clear?" Col asked Edeen and frowned up at Toren.

"The guardsmen still prowl the woods, but they are not what we need to fear."

Chapter Twenty

The world swayed. A steady heartbeat thumped against her ear. Charity blinked open her eyes and squinted through the pounding in her head. No, she was swaying. Or was it the forest's dark canopy above her?

She was in Toren's arms, her head resting on his shoulder, being carried through the woods. She nuzzled in closer, pushing her head beneath his chin, content to be in his arms. The residual stink of the dungeon didn't even bother her.

Except...? Why was he carrying her? He believed her to be one of Aldreth's lackeys.

She tried not to be mad at that. She really did. And she got it. Toren had been tortured by a woman for months. It wasn't his fault that he'd have trust issues, but really? He thought she'd work for someone like that? Except that was just it. He didn't know her. But he should because...bloody notion. She wasn't being fair.

Just because she'd gone through this instant emotional bond with him that was one of the most profound things that had ever happened to her in her life, she couldn't expect him to remember what had passed between them because for him it had never happened.

Her fault.

She'd taken that away herself when she used her grandmother's spell and traveled back a day through time and forever changed that moment, that glorious wonderful confusing moment between them, by not healing him.

Great. Hurray for her. She'd done it. She rode his time rift back in time and gotten him out of the dungeon just like she said she would. She got what she wanted, right?

So what did she expect?

That he would remember something that for him never happened? That when she healed him beneath the tangled branches, that deep connection they'd experienced before would miraculously occur again and he'd instantly feel something for her?

Well, okay, yes. Maybe she had expected that, but apparently that was a once in a lifetime happenstance.

Her lifetime.

Not his.

Her heart constricted. It was painful to breathe.

"Put me down," she said suddenly, squirming to get loose.

His hold tightened. "Cease. Ye'll hurt yourself."

"What do you care?"

She flopped out of his grasp forcefully enough that he let her slip away, though he did not fully let go until she was steady on her feet.

He frowned down at her and once again Charity was reminded of just how tall he was. His expression seemed almost, well, hurt. Edeen and Col came up behind him, watching.

"I do care," Toren's sultry voice whispered across her senses.

Charity went very still, uncertain.

He lifted his hand as though to reach out to her, but then dropped it.

She didn't know what to think, what to feel. Her pulse raced through her veins. She wanted to grab Toren's hand and just hang onto him, but wasn't certain what he was feeling toward her and couldn't take another accusation of working with Aldreth right now. Not now. Not while he was looking at her like he did when they were dream trailing. Like she was special to him. Like she meant something. She sent a questioning look to Edeen.

It was Col who came to her rescue. Taking her arm, he steered her away. "Are ye well enough, Charity?"

"I'm fine. Now. You're the one who fainted."

Col stopped mid-step, a scowl stamped across his lean features. "I did not faint."

"Flat on yer face. Swooned like a maiden," Edeen informed as she passed them.

"Did not. Warriors do not swoon." Col's long legs carried him to his sister.

Charity glanced back at Toren. His gaze remained steady on her, disconcerting. Not ready to talk with him, she walked on, feeling his eyes on her back.

A few hours later they came to a small river and Col announced happily, "We'll be on Limont land as soon as we cross the burn."

Charity nodded and plopped wearily to the damp edge of the river, startling only a little when Toren crouched beside her. It was a long river, surely he could have found another place to plant himself. He dipped low and began scooping water into his cupped palms and drinking lustfully. Charity couldn't help watching the way his Adam's apple bobbed in his strong throat column, satin skin moving over hard planes.

She looked away, eyeing the water, her own throat muscles working from thirst until Toren brought his hands to her, cupped together and brimming with tantalizing water. She quirked a brow at him. "Is it safe?"

His own brows pulled together in puzzlement. "Ye believe Aldreth has tainted it?"

No. Actually she was thinking more of the lack of purification tablets and parasites. It was a fairly strong current though and running water was safer than a still pond, right? At least she thought she'd heard that somewhere. How long would it take to boil it? The mercenaries wouldn't mind waiting. She was so thirsty. She looked Toren over again. He'd been drinking unpurified water his entire life and he was fit enough. Fit? He was beyond fit. Not in a body-builder type of way, but the long lean muscles built over a life actually engaging in activities that packed on muscle naturally. A working man, well, warrior. She was salivating.

For water. She was thirsty. Foregoing the water Toren held for her in his hands, she bent low and drank from her own hands. Gods, she didn't know water could taste so good. She gulped more and more.

Hands on her shoulders pulled her up. "Easy, lass, not so fast. Ye'll make yerself sick."

Uh, right. She grimaced at him, wiping her mouth, and shrugging his hands off until he got the message and let his hands fall. They sat in uncomfortable silence, taking small sips now and then. Col and Edeen's hushed chatter a little ways off filtered around them.

"Er." Toren cleared his throat. "Charity." She looked at him sidewise, suspicious at his uncharacteristic hesitancy. He wouldn't look at her, but stared into the tumbling river. "I..." he continued. "Ye have my gratitude."

Huh? She turned to fully face his profile. "Oh.

So you've decided I'm not an evil villain soul-bent on your destruction."

His lips quirked. "I never considered ye a villain."

"A pawn of a villain then, which is all the more insulting. If I wanted to, I'd make a great villain."

He faced her then, a full smile lifting his features and everything holding her spine together turned to goop. She actually swayed, but caught herself, freezing to the spot, as Toren's calloused hand brushed along her cheek and slipped into her hair. His face dipped close, inches from hers. "You could never be the villain," he crooned huskily before easing back.

Her spine tightened back up. Hard. Everything tightened. And tingled. Low. In parts she hadn't felt in a while. Her mouth went dry. Dang was she thirsty, but couldn't seem to turn toward the water lapping mere inches from her.

"I..." This wasn't fair. What he was doing to her. She was in to him. No doubt. She'd traveled centuries back through time just to help him and her body was reacting like a hormone-raging teenager just from a smile and husky voice. She had to clear the air, be up front, in order to keep her wits—and her hormones—in check enough to get through this ordeal. He had apologized for thinking she was working with Aldreth. Well, kind of. He hadn't said he was sorry, but he told her thank you. That was a start.

"Listen. Um, it's fine. Okay. I get it." She leaned back from him. Far back. He was still looking at her intensely and it was, well, intense. She swallowed. "You were hurt, feverish. How could you know who I was or what my intentions were. It's fine. It really is."

"I should have known," he said quietly and Charity's heart took a little stumble.

She went on quickly before her voice broke. "Look, I kind of messed-up your time-line a bit in order to get here. The first time, we um..." She dropped her gaze to her lap. "I healed you, and something happened, something..."

"Intimate?" he supplied for her and his voice caressed along her skin.

Heat poured into her cheeks as she nodded. "Y-yeah. We, um, shared..." She twirled her hands in the air between them as though she could erase the connection drawing her to him. "Bottom line, I feel things for you, all right." That's putting it mildly. "I wish I didn't. And I can't help it. You don't feel the same, which is fine. Really it is. I get it. You don't have to worry. I'm not some schoolgirl who is going to follow you around like an unwanted puppy. I'll get over it. Believe me I've done it before. So let's just get you to your clan, get these spelled bands off of you, and then you can open a rift and get me back home. You *can* get me back home, right?" She squinted up at him and darn if he didn't look a little disappointed.

His lips tightened and he dipped his head in a curt nod, long hair lowering in a jerk. "Once I have uninhibited use of my magic again, aye *Lady*, I can deliver ye to yer own time." That said, he rose and stalked off, hands clenched at his sides.

Chapter Twenty-One

Charity trudged up the forested hill, growing more despondent with each step. They had been walking for hours since crossing the river. She kept an eye on both men, gauging their exhaustion. Both had been through an ordeal and even with her healing, neither was at a hundred percent. Not that either would admit it. Then again, she didn't feel at top peak either.

Toren only slowed the pace when Col staggered though Charity had caught Toren listing a few times as well. He always caught himself and somehow rallied his strength. The dude was a machine.

She rolled her eyes, faulting the stubbornness of men regardless of what century they came from.

Speaking of…Charity wondered if Toren would really be able to send her back to her own time. He'd been through so much. What if he simply couldn't summon the ability anymore? Or it took him weeks to regain his strength. She could be stuck here for months.

Would that really be so bad? She wondered,

staring at his...oh what did it matter, she'd been watching his backside for hours. Admit it. He had a very nice backside.

So if she was stuck here for a while at least she'd have a nice view. And who knows, maybe the big lug could actually grow to like her somewhat.

They just had to get away from Aldreth. Which, if the witch could sense Toren's magic through the bands like he thought and could yank him right back. At any time. Why hadn't she done it already? Or shown up to get him? If she found Toren now, with the spelled bands on, he still wouldn't be a match for her Not without being able to use his magic against her. And Edeen and Col, as an empath and shapeshifter, wouldn't be able to fight against the magic of a witch of Aldreth's strength either.

What was she waiting for?

Thinking it through, she pushed between two trees that grew in a sort of lean as their roots grasped the side of the slope. Something didn't quite fit. It had been too easy so far. Their escape. Outrunning the guardsmen. The mercenaries would have to be bumbling idiots not to have seen their trail or catch up to them. Even she could track them and she had zero outdoor skills. There was nothing stopping Aldreth from just plucking Toren from them now. So why hadn't she?

"Charity?"

Friggincrapola. Bluidy, bluidy crap. Everything clicked into place.

"Charity." Edeen shook her shoulder.

Her head snapped up. "The mercenaries aren't trying to capture us. They're merely shadowing us. Maybe even herding us. Aldreth intends to take you and Col prisoner as well. We have to get those bands off Toren. Now."

Edeen's eyes narrowed as she studied her. "Ye and Toren, yer essences really are in accord." A dreamy look flitted across her features momentarily before tightening into determination. "He's come to the same conclusion, which is why we need to go." Grabbing her wrist, Edeen pulled her over the crest of the hill where the trees opened up onto an idyllic village below. Crops and pastures lay before them with long lines of short stone walls following pathways between them, leading around thatch-roofed cottages and joining to head up to a larger building that looked more like pictures of Viking longhouses than a Scottish keep.

As picturesque as the village appeared, something was off. Charity shaded her gaze with a steepled hand. Below, there was no movement. No sentries coming to greet or oppose them. There should be people in the fields, goats and sheep roaming about. The gates to the manor should not be sitting wide open. Well, at least she didn't think they should be.

"I thought we were going to the Shadowrood."

"Aye. We are." Toren's mouth settled into a hard line.

"The standing stones are not much farther," Col said. "We stopped here to make certain Shaw stood by his duty and took our people to the gateway, aye?"

"He's taken the clan to *Reolin Skene* without us then." Col's shoulders slumped. "When he found out Aldreth had spelled ye to the bands..." He looked at Charity in apology. "I wish he would have given us more time."

Frown lines creased Toren's forehead. "He did what needed to be done. 'Tis the course I would have plotted."

Charity backed away, horror squeezing her gut, Lenore's voice echoing in her head.

"It was a romantic story. An entire clan, every individual gifted with some form of magic as long as they remained the protectors of man... And then all of them vanished. Poof. The village must have fallen to ruin because no one knows where it once was."

Magic never has been the same in the world.

"Let's hurry. *Reolin Skene* is just on the other side of our village." Edeen started down the slope the way they had come. "Mayhap we're not too late."

Sharing a glance, Col and Toren followed after her.

Charity stood stock still.

She knew the outcome.

An entire clan, every individual gifted with some form of magic as long as they remained the protectors of man... And then all of them vanished...no one knows...

Either Shaw and the clan had already passed through, leaving the three remaining siblings on their own in the world. Or they would catch up and go into the Shadowrood with their clan.

All of them vanished.

The magic of the world is greatly lessened.

With the bands on or not, Aldreth would no longer be able to get to Toren in the Shadowrood.

But where would that leave her? Charity would be stuck in this time. Alone. With a whacked-out witch, seething that her own magic was no longer as strong without the clan of Limont in the world supporting it. Aldreth's magic, everyone's magic would be diminished to the point of barely there. Just like in her time where all magic wielders scraped by with what they could gather from the earth. On the up side, Aldreth would no longer have the magical means to wreak havoc upon mankind. That was a plus.

Before he entered the gateway, would there be time for Toren to send her back? Would he even be able to? In this time period, she had enough power on her own to lend him if he needed it, yet she was a healer. Only sorcerers had the necessary magic in them to open up a rift in time. Even Aldreth's witchy powers couldn't do that. Only Toren had the ability to get her home.

And then she'd never see him again.

She would never know if that connection they'd shared for even such a short time could be re-established.

He would never again look at her with wonder shining through his eyes. She wouldn't be around to see it.

Her heart thundered in her chest. Her breathing grew labored. Her breasts heaved against the material of her gown.

Toren had already started down. He turned back from lower on the hillside. He looked up at her, his expression different from any she'd yet seen him wear.

He stretched out his hand a little hesitant as though he was afraid she might not take it. He frowned, uncertain. "Come?"

Charity didn't know what to do. She would soon be on her own here.

She stared at Toren.

He didn't know her.

He didn't care for her, didn't feel any connection.

But she knew him.

She knew him.

She'd traversed his inner core, knew what was important to him, felt the depth of his love and loyalty, how he was willing to sacrifice all for his clan and family.

This was the same man she'd recklessly traveled through time for. The need to save him had overshadowed even common sense and she knew she would do it all over again.

Save him.

How could she not?

She loved him.

A shiver rolled down her arms.

Her vision blurred behind tears.

She loved him. And he didn't even know her.

But if she gave him a chance, maybe he would. In time.

Charity reached out her hand…

…and a blast of contained lightning knocked them both off their feet.

Chapter Twenty-Two

T hunder boomed and another jolt jagged of light sliced across the air.

A woman materialized at the crest of the hill. Sudden gusts snagged at her pitch-black hair and the white gown pressing against slender legs.

"Did ye believe I would not come for you?"

Aldreth glided down the slope, the ends of her gown trailing like smoke.

From the sloping ground, Charity pushed up to her arms. Her legs slid sideways on the incline. Across from her, Toren, too, pushed up, his head lifting as Aldreth stood above him. Charity's blood ran cold.

Dark storm clouds, purple like bruises, rolled overhead, gathering impossibly fast, violent and spitting lightning across the sky. Sparks lit the clouds from within while thunder rumbled through the charged atmosphere, heavy and thick and coated with ozone.

Struggling to his knees, Toren raised his arms. Purple tendrils of light lifted from his fingertips, cracking and hissing.

Aldreth threw back her head and laughed, hair streaming behind her. With a flick of her hand, the streamers of Toren's magic disappeared as though they'd never been. He could not use his magic against her.

Another flick of her wrist and he rolled through the air, landing with a jarring crunch where he slid down the slope.

Charity made it to her feet. Shrieking wind slammed her back down like she was a bird caught in a gale force. Her hair flew in front of her face and then streamed back again, pulling at her scalp. She lunged up like a sprinter. Flapping skirts tangled around her legs. She had to get to Toren. Soil slid under her precarious steps.

Planting her feet, she leaned into the slope, hanging onto rocks and thin slanted trees to make her way down.

Another bolt of magic hit Toren. His back arched off the ground, body spasming. Aldreth's hands danced and he sailed across the slope. The witch manipulated him like a puppet master. Toren tried to lunge up and his feet swept out from under him.

The winds howled, tossing dirt and debris at Charity. She tumbled the last few feet to the bottom of the ravine. Footfalls ran past her, flinging dirt in her hair. Charity rolled to her side to see what was happening. Edeen launched herself at the witch, arm stretched out. Her hand hit the spot above Aldreth's heart.

Both women screamed. Their bodies stiffened, convulsing like they'd been caught in an electrical stream. Whatever Edeen was doing as an empath, it was hurting the witch. It was hurting Edeen too.

Aldreth's features twisted horribly.

Edeen's eyes rolled up in her head until only the whites showed.

"Nooooo!" Col raced forward. There was an explosion of golden light. Col vanished. In his place, a dark panther leaped out of the brilliance, snarling teeth and claws that rammed between the women, throwing them apart. Both women dropped boneless to the ground.

Charity lunged up.

The panther spun back, soil flying beneath his unsheathed claws. Aldreth threw out an arm. A lash of lightning hit Col, tossing him with such force his glossy side plowed up the hill, gouging a thick furrow in the ground.

Aldreth dragged herself to her feet, her eyes wild. What had Edeen done to her? The witch threw out her arms. The air crackled, the force of tremendous magic building like a volcano about to erupt.

A lightning bolt plowed across the ground, hitting Toren square in the chest. He flew backward.

This had to stop.

Charity ran toward Aldreth.

"You witch!" She cold-cocked her right in the kisser.

Aldreth went down. Her legs flew up. She blinked up at her, wide-eyed, from the ground. Slowly, she wiped blood from her split lip.

Charity winced. Her hand throbbed.

Aldreth rose. "So ye're the Healer Enchantress who has kept Toren's spirits from failing him." Her gaze roamed down the length of Charity with as much interest as if she was inspecting an ant. "Hmmm." She shot out an arm and Charity flew back as though she'd been struck by a log.

Toren screamed out her name.

Head ringing, flat on her back, Charity blinked up at the angry spitting skies. Shallow breaths pulled in and out of her lungs.

"Nay, Aldreth, do not." Toren cried. For her.

Darkness moved over her. Aldreth's slim form blotted out the sky as she stood over her. The hem of her white dress flapped across Charity's stomach.

Aldreth's head cocked to the side. Her swollen broken mouth twitched in a hard smile. "'Tis an omen, ye're being brought here, that all I've attempted is just and right."

Aldreth leaned closer over her. Her long hair tickled Charity's face as the wind whipped it back and forth. Charity tried to pull in a breath, gasping instead. The witch's eyes blazed, dilated with magic and madness. "At long last I have the means to break Toren." She pulled Charity up by her hair. Pain radiated through her. She twisted to escape it, hands clutched on Aldreth's wrists to take some of the pressure off her tearing hair.

"Stop it!" Suddenly Toren was there, arms around the witch, pulling her away.

Charity dropped. The pressure on her scalp was immediately gone.

The air exploded, a vicious concussion of tearing sound.

Crying out, Toren dropped to the ground where Aldreth turned on him, punching out crimson light that slapped into the sorcerer. His hands clawed into the soil, every muscle rigid with strain.

A panther shrieked. Col sprang through the air. Aldreth spun. A gash of light knocked Col sideways.

Another ripped into Toren.

Unable to use his magic against her, Toren was vulnerable, helpless, just a man, beneath the enormity of her power.

Aldreth blasted Toren again. Again.

In her fury, she was going to kill him.

Still in panther form, Col leapt at them again. A bolt of charged fire slashed him in the face. It caught him up in a stream of light, kept him frozen in the air, his sleek form bending and writhing, fur standing on end.

Behind him, Toren staggered to get to his feet.

"No!" A shout growled across the hill.

An incredible wave of power pulsed through everything, pierced into Charity like water through a net, warm and hard with the promise of creating a hundred worlds or destroying a million others flooded in its strength. A whisper of darkness sifted through it. Mountains fell to dust. Oceans swallowed continents. Entire cities crumbled. She'd never felt anything like it.

The storm abruptly stilled. Col dropped to the ground, steam lifting off his fur.

Toren lay unmoving.

Shaw stood at the bottom of the hill, between them and the abandoned village, his expression a mixture of devastation and horror at what he had just unleashed. His eyes glowed silver white, reflecting the shine of a trillion moons.

Charity sensed even Shaw had no idea of the full extent of his power, yet there wasn't a magic wielder within miles who wouldn't have felt the depth of what he'd just revealed. The ferocious potency breathed upon the very air.

Toren's head lifted. Shock and horror deepened the lines of his forehead.

Aldreth turned toward Shaw, undisguised

wonder stark upon her features. "You. It should have been you all along." Her chest heaved in and out and her eyes rolled up in what Charity could only describe as arousal. "I can feel the darkness within you." She held out a palm. "Come to me. Ye and I are alike."

Shaw's gun-metal eyes narrowed. He started up the slope. "Leave this place, Aldreth. Be gone and never return."

Aldreth let her arm drop. She smiled. "Ye're strong, but ye're also young. I've had centuries to hone my craft." She glided over to where the panther lay unmoving, crouched down and petted his fur.

Shaw froze. His chest expanded on a ragged breath.

A low growl emitted from the panther's throat. He swiped out a weak claw, ripping through Aldreth's pristine gown. Lines of blood sprouted at her hip.

Enraged, Aldreth slammed her fist into Col's side and the panther screamed. Light sparked and the large cat dispersed. A naked battered Col took his place, curling into himself. Veins stood stark white in his rigid hands and arms.

Shaw's blast rolled into Aldreth. His eyes blazed silver light. Releasing Col, she flung her arms out toward Shaw and their magic collided.

Though she could not see Shaw's force with her eyes, Charity felt it with every fiber of her being. It was like being near a roaring waterfall, feeling the strength and energy of it rumbling through the ground and air as it spilled over the edge.

The clouds swirled above them, buffeting in roaring force. The ground groaned beneath them. Dirt and pebbles shook, bouncing off the ground, rolling into small landsides.

Holes ripped open in the air, time rifts jarred apart, seething and sputtering charged matter into the atmosphere. That should not be able to happen. A witch should not be able to open a rift. And a... Charity stared at Shaw. His hair floated upward, wild streams of black. She hadn't a clue what Shaw really was or what his magic was capable of. Moon Sifter. Could he open rifts in time or was it a combination of the magic he and Aldreth were generating in the atmosphere?

In her rage, Aldreth had gone mad, shooting

out her magic in every direction.

And her magic was immense.

Trees uprooted.

Boulders rolled down the hill.

Edeen's unconscious form slid farther down the slope toward the maelstrom Shaw and Aldreth unleashed upon each other.

Col lifted his head, rousing.

Toren staggered to his feet.

Aldreth moved down the hill, thrusting everything she had at Shaw, shots of gilded lightning executed with the precision of a surgeon.

Shaw stumbled back.

Aldreth screamed at him. "Yer brother, the most powerful sorcerer in the land couldn't fight me. Do ye really believe an unskilled child as yerself has a chance?"

One of Shaw's legs buckled and he fell on a knee. Sweat poured down his face. Huge tremors rolled through him. His dark swirled and tangled behind him. If this was the first time he'd tapped into his potential, the effort would be overpowering. He'd had no training. There'd been no one capable of training him. Even if his magic was stronger, no way could he keep pulling from it. The physical toll on him had to be enormous, yet Aldreth appeared to be having no such issues.

Another time rift tore open behind him, angry and unstable.

"I'll have what is in you, Shaw Limont, and then I'll wield the balance of yer entire pitiful clan."

Shaw's head snapped up. He smiled, a triumphant slash of white in the darkness. "Ye may have me, but my clan has crossed into the Shadowrood."

Somewhere close, Toren groaned.

Shaw's gaze sought his brother's and his smile turned apologetic. "They're safe. The clan is beyond reach and their magic with them. The Fae have bound the gateway."

"No!" Aldreth shouted. "What have ye done? Ye've ruined everything! They cannot be gone. What have ye done?"

Twisting her body, she pulled her arms back to the side and swung back like an orchestra conductor. Giant crackling light pooled around her hands and then flew out toward Shaw.

A blur dove between them. Col took the hit and

the angry light flung him across the air. He sailed backwards into the time rift and disappeared.

Chapter Twenty-Three

S haw, Toren, and Charity cried out as one.

Col, no. He couldn't be gone!

Roaring, Shaw threw everything he had at Aldreth. Momentarily stunned, she reeled back, but quickly recovered and pummeled Shaw beneath successive streaks of magic.

The young man was taking a beating, thrown to the ground, head and shoulders snapping to and fro as though hit by an unseen fist. He doubled over, hands and knees hit the ground just before he was flipped onto his back.

Aldreth was killing him and no one had the strength to stop her. Charity pulled up to her knees. Wobbled. Every muscle in her body felt like she had just finished a major workout.

Through the corner of her eye, she saw Toren run forward and was shoved back by the waves of magic coming off of Shaw like a backdraft.

Toren was a powerful and skilled enough sorcerer to fight Aldreth. Charity had felt the strength of his core. She believed in him, but he could not use his magic against Aldreth.

He could not use *his* magic because of the horrible spelled bands.

Charity gasped and shoved to her feet again.

He can't use his magic upon Aldreth, but maybe he could use hers.

Before, when they'd used their magic together, Charity had drawn from Toren's reservoirs. First, when she had healed him and then the second time when she'd tapped into his magic to have enough to send her back to his time period.

Here. Now. In this century, she had ten times as much magic of her own to rely on. Why couldn't Toren draw from her reservoir that was untouched by Aldreth's spell?

Fueled by a new surge of adrenaline, Charity raced to Toren's side. He was on his feet, once more, fighting past the backlash of streaming magic to get to his remaining brother.

Charity grabbed his arm and without an explanation, focused everything she had to pour into him. She had no idea if this would work.

His face swung to hers and then dipped to her hand at the rosy light pooling around her fingertips. His eyes widened, brows rose.

"Take it," she gritted out. "Use it against her."

His jaw clenched. Message received.

Toren's hand slipped over hers. Magic roared out of her in a heady rush. She swayed, felt herself lowered to her knees, Toren's hand still gripped over hers, his arm at her waist.

Everything she was melted into him. Events replayed across her sight like a reel-to-reel projector running backwards.

The flight through the forest, Col's light energy form stretched across the doorway, finding Toren in the dungeon, being carried over Shaw's shoulder, kneeling in her kitchen above a wounded Toren, slipping into his dream, back in the kitchen—the first time—using her magic to heal him, their magic weaving together, connecting them as one, the bonding...

And wham! It was back.

That connection, all that feeling, knowing another person inside and out, almost better than she knew herself...

"Charity." He spoke her name like a fragile spell so weak the smallest breath might make it unravel.

She looked up into his face and saw it all there in an expression of wonder.

Her frozen heart stormed back to life.

Toren smiled and nodded. Hands clasped, together they stood to face Aldreth, and Charity felt Toren stir her magic, shaping it into something new, something beyond the ability to heal, something lethal and focused.

His arms flung out, bringing Charity's with his and a blinding spear of tourmaline light flew from between their clasped palms and...nothing.

The magic shot out, she saw the purple streak, but then it was as though it poured into water and dissolved like sugar.

Aldreth looked over her shoulder at them, smiled, and resumed her assault on Shaw.

Not knowing what else to do, Charity grabbed onto Toren's wrist to try and undo the spell just as Edeen had tried before. She had no idea what the spell was, but she had to try something.

Toren shifted up. He was going to tackle Aldreth physically again. He'd never make it. The witch would kill him with one blast. She'd gone mad, was out of her head. But she was killing Shaw too. Charity pulled back on Toren's wrist, keeping him grounded, at the same time pushing all her senses into the band, searching for the puzzle to undo the spell.

She felt the powerful spell used to lock it to Toren. It was a combination of blackness and evil, power imbued from demonic essences, riddled with death. It hurt to touch it. No wonder Toren couldn't escape its magic.

Who was she kidding? It would take her months to figure this out. Her talent did not lend itself to picking apart a crazy witch's dark spell. Her gift was healing.

Healing.

Time seemed to slow. Charity pulled forth her gift, her magic to heal and let it flow into the band. Without looking, she grabbed onto Toren's other wrist, sensing exactly where his hand was. Toren was still pulling away from her, but his movements were slow. No, time was slowing, everything distilled down to this one moment, this one happening. Healing magic spread into the bands, into the dark spell, flowing over the blackness like spilled wine. Her magic did not unravel the spell.

Her magic healed it. It drew out the darkness the same as she would squeeze pus from an infected wound, drawing it out, out, away, and let it dissipate into the roiling angry air. Like seeks like. And when she was done, her magic withdrew, leaving the spell still a spell, but unrecognizable—a benign useless thing.

The bands shriveled and fell from Toren's wrists.

Time resumed its natural speed.

And Charity met Toren's awed gaze.

He took her hand, lifting their palms once more, and spewed out an enormous blast of blue-violet light that roared into Aldreth's back.

The witch's hand flew up. The punishment she'd been pounding into Shaw sputtered and zoomed up into the sky.

The young warrior listed sideways on his knees and slumped to the ground.

Aldreth fell forward to her hands and knees. She twisted around. A dark eyebrow arched. She glanced at their joined hands with disdain and shook her head.

She stood up slowly and somewhat shakily

and smoothed her hair back down. "I weary of these games. Come with me, Toren. Give me yer magic and I'll let what's left of yer family live." Her gaze slanted to Charity. "I'll also allow ye to keep yer pretty plaything as a pet." She shook out her gown. "After all, yer clan is gone. 'Twill just be you and I." She smiled. "And yer brother. He has hidden what he is all these years. I'll enjoying unraveling his secrets."

Toren's arm tensed along Charity's.

Aldreth looked down at Shaw. "We can salvage what's left of our magic together. With yer clan taken from the world, all magic will fade. Can ye feel it lessening already? Surely ye do not want to live a life without magic? Come with me. Together we'll retain what we can."

Geez. Charity scowled. The chick didn't know when to give up. Lady, you've been rejected. Get over it. "I don't think so."

Aldreth's face hardened. Her hands lifted.

And Toren zapped her off her feet. "Ye've brought enough ruin to this world."

His magic spilled through Charity, undiluted and heady. Apparently they were still joined somehow. Together, she and Toren were formidable.

He zapped Aldreth again. With the bands gone, Toren's magic was no longer restrained, yet he had not gone in for the kill.

Aldreth's face crumpled, finally catching on to the danger.

Toren moved forward, bringing Charity with him, entwined hands outstretched.

Aldreth scrambled to the other side of Shaw and pulled his limp body up to shield her. Shaw groaned. His head lolling, arms dangling.

"Aldreth…" Toren warned. "Let him go."

"You would not give me what is rightfully mine, but he will. We are not finished, you and I, Toren Limont." Aldreth ran a hand through Shaw's dark hair and smiled. "Worry not. I will take the utmost care with him. As I did for ye." She pressed her lips to Shaw's temple and in a brilliant flash, they were gone.

Toren ran to the empty spot they'd just occupied and slashed a fist through the air. "Shaw!"

Epilogue

Toren carried his unconscious sister into their deserted village, past the thatched longhouse and into a small cottage that Charity assumed belonged to Edeen. He placed her gently on the bed and stood back, scrubbing a palm down his face. Charity's heart wept for him. He'd endured Aldreth's tortures for months, not giving in solely to keep his clan and family safe.

Now it seemed his brothers and sister were lost to him regardless.

Toren stepped away from the quilted bed like a boy afraid his clumsiness might break something important. He turned glossy eyes to Charity. "Can ye...?"

"Of course." She crossed the room to him and squeezed his arm. She felt like she'd run a marathon, legs were rubber, back unbendable, but she wanted Edeen well and whole as much as Toren did. "I'll do what I can."

She sat on the side of the bed, taking in the girl's still features, the slow rise and fall of her chest and pushed her fear over what happened to Shaw and Col to the back of her heart so that she could concentrate solely on helping Edeen.

Placing a palm over Edeen's sternum, Charity pulled from her own essence and allowed the energy to heal flow outward.

The familiar light sparkled at her fingertips, comforting and warm and sank into the girl, seeking injury, something out of the ordinary.

She searched long and hard, exhaustion trying to pull her back, which only made her press harder to find something, any trace of magic that was neither Edeen's or her own, any hint to why she remained unconscious, to what had happened between Edeen and the witch on that awful hill.

As an empath, there should be myriad traces of magic to sift through…yet, there was none.

What had happened when Edeen had latched onto Aldreth's magic in full swing? It was as though the witch's force had backlashed into Edeen and shorted her out.

Charity felt herself drifting out of the girl's essence. She fell into strong arms.

A handsome anxious face blurred into her

vision. "Are ye all right? Charity, look at me."

Pressing a hand to her rioting head, she nodded. "I'm okay."

Toren held her up off the rush-covered floor where she must have sloshed over. Edeen remained still and unmoving on the bed.

Charity met Toren's pain-filled gaze. She could tell he was afraid to ask what she'd learned. She brought her hands up to cup his face. "She merely sleeps, Toren." She wanted so badly to comfort him. "She has not been harmed. Not in any way that I can tell. She's okay...just asleep."

"Then why will she not awaken?"

"I don't know." Charity shook her head. "She's deep." She wasn't sure exactly how to explain what she'd felt. "Edeen's personality, her essence, who she is, has sunk way down deep where—"

"Where ye cannot reach her." The Adam's apple in Toren's throat column bounced.

"No. I can't," she whispered. "But I will. I'll figure out a way. I won't stop trying. We'll get her back, Toren. I'm not going back home until we figure out how to help Edeen."

Toren stared at her for a long while until

something indefinable about his expression changed. She couldn't quite place what, for his features were still etched with worry, yet hope had somehow seeped into his being. She felt it radiating off of him. "Ye're willing to stay?"

She nodded, the weight of what she was doing falling like raindrops around her, soaking into the hardened ground. "Edeen is my friend. I won't abandon her."

"As ye would not abandon me." The pads of his fingers traced along her cheek, trailing warmth. "Ye said ye would save me. And ye did. I believe you, Charity Healer Enchantress beyond Time. I believe you. Ye say we will save my sister, I believe you."

Several emotions spread through Charity's breast, too many to sort through. She stared into Toren's eyes, held captive by the full strength of his trust and hope and belief. Belief in her. That connection, that truly knowing and understand another, was back and streaming powerfully between them. Her heart pulled, thumping heavily against her ribs in rhythm with his. Gods, she loved him.

His trust in her made her believe it herself. They could help Edeen. After all, they had already conquered time together. And they'd broken the witch's bands. Together they could do anything.

Charity smiled, hope blossoming warmth throughout her essence. "We'll get her back, Toren. We'll get them all back."

Toren nodded, a tear spilled down his cheek. "I believe you. We will. Together. We'll awaken Edeen and we will discover where time has swept Col. We *will* find him and bring him back to us." He kissed Charity's forehead. "Charity, I..." His face filled with wonder. "I remember. I do not how 'tis possible, but I remember two events one upon the other."

She felt tears wet her cheeks. "I know. I felt it."

"Then ye know the depth of my feelings for you." His voice came out strong like the force of the tide that pulled Charity under with it. "I do not wish for you to *get over me*," he repeated the words she had thrown at him.

Her heart swelled with love for the lug, her Highlander that she'd risk traveling through time to save. "I—" But she didn't get to answer, because

Toren's mouth pressed over hers, showing exactly what he felt, leaving no room for doubt. Heat buzzed through her. Her senses exploded with it. Their magic flared, tangling together with an ebb and flow uniquely their own, together as though their very souls, their essences demanded to be forever entwined.

Toren pulled back, leaving her lungs pulling in shallow breaths. Her lips felt swollen, thoroughly kissed and yearning for more of the same.

He set her back, seeming unnerved as though to kiss her again just now would take away all reason and he needed to remain in control. They had work to do.

He shook his head and pushed back his hair, his face ruddy with need, his eyes darker somehow and Charity's stomach took an oh-so-slow little somersault.

The throat muscles in Toren's neck bounced. And bounced again. "We will find Col, get him back," he resumed. "And Shaw..."

Shaw was much more complicated. They'd seen the broken defeat in his expression. With the clan gone and the darkness inside him...Charity feared the young man may have already lost the will to resist Aldreth.

The fragile hope between them plummeted. Charity lowered her head, once again giving into fear and worry.

It was Toren who bolstered her courage this time. He lifted her chin to meet his gaze.

"I will not leave my brother to the witch." An unspoken question burned in his eyes. Was she with him in this also? Going against the witch again would not be easy. Especially not that she knew what power lay between them.

Charity smiled grimly and took his hand. "Nor will I, Toren. Nor will I."

The adventures for the guardians of the balance of magic has just begun. Find out what happens to Edeen in *Highland Empath*.

Become one of Clover's Lucky Charmers for bonus insights and to be the first to know when the newest books are out.

ABOUT THE AUTHOR

Clover Autrey writes the kind of stories she loves to read, high fantasy and time travels with Scottish Highlanders or magical mermen and shapeshifters, with powerful elements of romance, where the hero and heroine must each make sacrifices to gain something even stronger. She is the author of the HIGHLAND SORCERY series and the ANOINTED series.

Clover serves as the current president of the Keller Writers Association and is the past president of North Texas Romance Writers of America. She is a frequent speaker at conferences and workshops.

Inspired by her love of Louis L'Amour historical romantic heroes, Clover (yeah, that's her real name), packed up and moved to Texas where she found a real live Texan of her own. She's been there ever since where she and Pat (who else would a Clover marry but a Patrick?) listen to the coyotes howl at the trains each evening.

Connect with her at cloverautrey.com

Made in the USA
Middletown, DE
07 January 2022